Cam pushe ~~~~ **to the bedroom and watched Lily's sleeping form on the bed.**

He studied the now-calm features that had been nothing but stressed and tense since the moment she'd first walked into the precinct.

Cam reached for the blanket Lily had draped across a chair, unfolded the fleece and spread it over her, letting his fingertips trail across her shoulder, reaching to brush the hair from her face.

Then he did something he hadn't done in some time. He crawled into bed next to a woman. More aptly, he crawled on top of the bed, on top of the blanket, but he reached for her, enfolding Lily into his arms. She moved closer, tucking against his body as if she knew he wanted nothing more than to keep her safe.

Yet as the warmth of Lily's body permeated the cold recesses of Cam's heart, he knew he no longer had to worry about crossing the line between professional and personal.

He had only to worry about how to cross back.

KATHLEEN LONG

COLD CASE CONNECTION

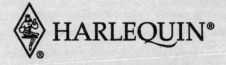

HARLEQUIN®

TORONTO • NEW YORK • LONDON
AMSTERDAM • PARIS • SYDNEY • HAMBURG
STOCKHOLM • ATHENS • TOKYO • MILAN • MADRID
PRAGUE • WARSAW • BUDAPEST • AUCKLAND

To Koula—friend and reader extraordinaire—
with gratitude and love.

ISBN-13: 978-0-373-69327-6
ISBN-10:   0-373-69327-3

COLD CASE CONNECTION

ABOUT THE AUTHOR

After a career spent spinning words for clients ranging from corporate CEOs to talking fruits and vegetables, Kathleen now finds great joy spinning a world of fictional characters, places and plots. Having decided to pursue her writing goals when her first daughter taught her that life is short and dreams are for chasing, Kathleen is now the award-winning author of breathtaking romantic suspense for Harlequin Intrigue.

A RIO Award of Excellence winner and a National Readers Choice, Booksellers Best and Holt Medallion nominee, her greatest reward can be found in the letters and e-mails she receives from her readers. Nothing makes her happier than knowing one of her stories has provided a few hours of escape and enjoyment, offering a chance to forget about life for a little while.

Along with her husband, daughter, and one very neurotic sheltie, Kathleen divides her time between suburban Philadelphia and the New Jersey seashore, where she can often be found hands on keyboard—bare toes in sand—spinning tales. After all, life doesn't get much better than that.

Please visit her at www.kathleenlong.com or drop her a line at P.O. Box 3864, Cherry Hill, NJ 08034.

Books by Kathleen Long

HARLEQUIN INTRIGUE
847—SILENT WARNING
914—WHEN A STRANGER CALLS
941—WITHOUT A DOUBT
959—RELUCTANT WITNESS
976—A NECESSARY RISK
993—HIGH SOCIETY SABOTAGE
1054—POSITIVE I.D.*
1060—COLD CASE CONNECTION*

*The Body Hunters

CAST OF CHARACTERS

Lily Christides—A member of The Body Hunters, she's traveled home to Philadelphia to find her sister Nicole's true killer, no matter how tidy the local police force thinks the case may be.

Cameron Hughes—Part of the team that originally convicted serial killer Buddy Grey, he's convinced Nicole died because she freed a guilty man. He'll do whatever it takes to put Grey back behind bars.

Nicole Christides—The up-and-coming reporter was murdered on the heels of her biggest exclusive—setting convicted killer Buddy Grey free. Did she truly believe the man to be innocent? Or did she set a murderer free in order to grab the headlines?

Buddy Grey—Released from jail after serving time for a trio of murders, did he murder Nicole? Or has his signature style been borrowed by a killer whose identity has yet to be determined?

Tim Fitzsimmons—The head of the city's urban redevelopment program and Nicole's grieving boyfriend, had he pursued the reporter out of true attraction? Or was his interest based on a motive far more sinister?

Tracey Sizemore—She vanished from summer camp nineteen years earlier. Will the mystery of her past be the key to unlocking the tangled clues of the present?

The Body Hunters—Will Connors, Rick Matthews, Kyle Landenburg, Silvia Hellman and Martin Booker—Dedicated to finding victims and villains society has abandoned, they'll use every means necessary to find Nicole's killer. The Body Clock is ticking.

Prologue

Nicole Christides reached for her ringing cell phone and glanced at the caller's name. Her sister, Lily. She grinned. "So let me get this straight. Mom and Dad go on a cruise and I get promoted to being the target of your weekly guilt call?"

"It's not a guilt call." Lily's voice tightened defensively.

"Oh, yes, it is." Nicole didn't do a thing to hide her laughter. She shrugged, even though her sister had no way of seeing the move. "So you moved to the opposite coast. They'll get over it."

"Easy for you to say, you're the star daughter."

"Speaking of which—" Nicole checked her reflection in the foyer mirror and frowned "—I'm meeting with one of the network execs in thirty and I've got to freshen up."

Lily snapped her tongue and Nicole winced. Her younger sister had never had to voice her disapproval of anything. All she had to do was snap her tongue and her point had been made.

"I really do have a meeting," Nicole insisted.

"Sure you do."

She knew her family was proud of her work as a local

television reporter, but they were also proud of Lily. Lily, however, didn't see things that way.

Why Nicole's sister had chosen crunching numbers over a profession that would showcase her natural beauty and brains was beyond Nicole, but she'd learned a long time ago never to question Lily or her motives.

As for Nicole, her recent work to free convicted killer Buddy Grey had made her a household name and garnered media attention—a *lot* of media attention. Her newly found popularity hadn't escaped the notice of the higher-ups.

Tonight's meeting would more than likely be her ticket up and out of the Philadelphia market.

"You're going to tell me you don't have a second to talk to your sister?" Lily asked.

The doorbell chimed and Nicole reached for the doorknob without a glance at the peephole.

"Hang on, Lil. Someone's at the door."

A deliveryman stood on the top step of the brownstone's entrance, cap pulled low over his eyes. The huge basket of flowers he cradled in one arm blocked most of his face.

All thoughts of safety flew out of Nicole's head at the sight of the beautiful arrangement.

"*Flowers.* I'll call you back, Lil."

She flipped her phone shut, disconnecting her call before her sister could say another word.

The man at the door lowered the basket and took a forward step. The sudden motion startled Nicole and she looked at the man's face, recognition coming in a slow haze of disbelief. "What on earth are you doing delivering flowers?"

He smiled a cold, calculated smile. Nicole blinked, working to wrap her brain around the fact he'd shown up on her front step.

He closed the space between them, and an inexplicable sense of dread gripped her as she took a backward step.

"To what do I owe the pleasure—"

He dropped the flowers and backhanded her before she could finish the question.

Pain exploded across her cheekbone and the phone dropped from her fingers, springing open as it hit the floor. Nicole fell against the wall, grasping frantically at the woodwork for anything to hang on to, anything that would help her pull away from him before he could hit her again.

He knotted one hand into her hair and jerked her backward, his fingers wrapping around her throat even as she struggled to get a hand beneath his, to break the vise around her neck.

Her gaze landed on the cell phone.

All she had to do was hit the call back button and Lily would hear what was happening. She'd get help.

Nicole struggled in vain, frantically working to break her attacker's hold on her neck. But the more she fought, the tighter he pressed, both hands wrapped around her throat, choking her, squeezing all conscious thought from her brain.

The cell phone rang and her attacker momentarily stilled.

Nicole kicked and flailed her arms, trying to connect with the phone, the man's face or body, anything.

Her heel hit the phone, but the ringing stopped. Hopelessness washed through her.

She was too late. Too slow.

Whoever had been on the other end of the line would never hear her now.

The man tightened his hands around her throat and her vision dimmed. She fought to form a plan, but thought failed her.

In the last moment before she slid into unconsciousness, her attacker pressed his lips to her ear and spoke.

"I'm about to give you the biggest headline of your career. Pity you won't be alive to see it."

LILY CHRISTIDES.

The Man took a sip of his bourbon and thought again of the name he'd read on Nicole Christides's phone. The second call had come after the life had left the reporter's body, but he needed silence to concentrate on the rest of his work.

He'd powered off the phone before he'd tucked it into his pocket. Then he'd finished his handiwork. His masterpiece.

Who was Lily Christides? A sister? A cousin?

He scowled.

Nicole's phone had been open when the first call came, yet during their struggle the ringing had stopped. The now-dead reporter had kicked the phone into the wall a moment later, snapping the tiny object shut.

Was there a chance the first call had been answered while the phone was open?

Had the caller heard anything The Man had said?

He shook off the ridiculous thought and patted the pocket where he'd tucked Nicole's phone. He had nothing to worry about. Fate had surely smiled on him as it always had.

Yet, he slipped the phone from his pocket and powered it on just the same. One voice mail waiting. Christides, no doubt.

He pulled up the call menu and the list of missed calls expecting two from the Christides number. Instead, the screen displayed only one.

"Damn."

He moved to the received call menu and there it was.

The first Christides call had connected, allowing fifteen seconds of open air. Had the caller overheard the words he'd whispered in Nicole's ear?

If she had, his careful work might be for nothing.

He'd used a vacuum identical to the ones crime scene technicians wielded in order to eliminate trace evidence.

He'd carefully gathered up the floral basket and the petals that had dropped, leaving not so much as a spec of pollen behind.

The Man wrapped his fingers around the phone and squeezed.

Lily Christides.

The young woman sitting at the end of the bar laughed, and he glanced in her direction. She sat head lowered, her focus glued to the cell phone in her hand. She tapped in a message, tucking a loose strand of sleek blond hair behind her ear as she smiled.

He gestured to the bartender. "Another bourbon—" he jerked a thumb in the young woman's direction "—and refill whatever it is she's drinking."

After all, the least he could do was buy her a drink.

He scrolled through the menu choices on Nicole's phone until he found what he wanted. Then he pulled the number for Lily Christides from the contact list.

Nicole lived alone, didn't work weekends and was currently dating the head of the city's urban revitalization program, in Vegas until Sunday night at a conference. The Man had only to read the newspaper to learn that much.

With any luck at all, no one would find the reporter's body for at least forty-eight hours, especially if no one suspected anything of being wrong.

He keyed in a text message and hit Send.

Sorry about tonight. Call you tomorrow.

That ought to keep everyone worry free for a while.

And worry free was exactly what The Man intended to be for a long, long time to come.

Chapter One

Philadelphia homicide detective Cameron Hughes didn't know who he was more pissed off at. The prosecutor's crack team of lawyers who'd mucked up his case seven years earlier, or the body lying in the middle of the kitchen.

Nicole Christides.

She'd no doubt been murdered by Buddy Grey as some sort of sick thank you for her work in overturning the conviction Cam had busted his hump for years earlier.

She'd last been seen at the news station a bit before five o'clock tonight. They'd found her body thanks to an over-zealous assistant who went looking for the star reporter after she failed to show for a meeting with a network executive.

Cam directed a sharp nod at the nearest crime-scene technician. "Anything?"

The young man pursed his lips. "Nothing obvious. Won't know until I process everything. The place is so clean I'd swear someone's already done this." He nodded toward the vacuum in his hand.

Cam glared at the small vacuum used for gathering trace evidence. He already knew what they'd find back at the lab. Nothing.

Grey was too careful. He was too smart. With the exception of the one time he'd left a hair behind on a victim.

A single hair Cam had used to nail the case that should have put the man away forever.

The prosecutor's office had broken the chain of custody, flushing Grey's guilty verdict down the toilet thanks to crack reporter Nicole Christides.

Cam stole a quick glance at her battered body and groaned.

He raked a hand across his face and stepped back out of the kitchen. He'd never been a fan, but no one deserved to die like this. Not even a pain-in-the-neck reporter with nothing better to do than set serial killers free.

"You'll call me as soon as you're done processing the scene?"

"Will do." The tech's voice trailed Cam as he headed into the brownstone's center hall toward the victim's office.

Cam patted his pocket, longing for the cigarettes he'd given up three years earlier. Instead he found the ever-present pack of gum he carried to fill the void of craving his nasty habit had left behind.

He unwrapped a piece, folded the sugary stick into his mouth and waited for a sense of comfort that never came.

The homicide response team moved through the victim's brownstone with a precision choreographed by years of practice and experience. Outside, the strobe lights of emergency vehicles filled the night, matched only by the glare of television and newspaper cameras.

A throng of reporters swarmed the sidewalk and street, waiting for word on the fate of one of their own, no doubt hoping for the darkest, grittiest, most sensational headline possible.

Cam wasn't sure of a lot in life, but at that moment he was sure of two things.

The reporters outside were not going to be disappointed.

And he and his team were in for a long, long night.

LILY CHRISTIDES STARED OUT the window at the Philadelphia skyline as the pilot announced the plane's descent.

As part of her covert work with a group of private individuals known as The Body Hunters, she had to be willing to drop her life at a moment's notice to respond to the ticking clock of a new case.

The Body Clock, they called it. A tool The Body Hunters used in their searches for missing victims or at-large criminals.

Never had she dreamed the clock would be ticking for her sister's killer. She brushed a fresh round of tears from beneath her eyes and did her best to focus on the facts of her sister's murder and not the emotions.

Even though she'd recently been on assignment on Isle de Cielo, Lily had caught the news of Buddy Grey's release from Graterford Prison.

The police had apparently chosen Grey as their number one person of interest in Nicole's murder. The method matched the earlier crimes to a tee, yet Lily wasn't buying the theory.

Nicole was too smart to have been killed by Grey. She'd believed in the man's innocence. She never would have worked to free him otherwise.

Nicole had proven the prosecutor's office mishandled evidence in the trio of murders for which Grey had been sent to death row. She'd made the rounds on local and national television and radio, not to mention the five-part exposé her station had run on the eleven o'clock news. Their mother had recorded and sent the entire series to Lily in Seattle.

Lily blew out a sigh, silently acknowledging the competition that had simmered between the two sisters for as long as she could remember.

Maybe she'd been jealous because she couldn't brag to the world about the cases she'd worked, the missing persons she'd located, families she'd helped reunite or closure her work had provided. Truth was, none of that mattered now.

None of it.

Her sister was dead, and life would never be the same.

Lily thought again about their conversation and her attempts to call Nicole back.

She'd been so focused on the fact Nicole had given her the brush-off that her sister's last words hadn't fully registered. Nicole had said she'd call Lily back, but was there something else?

The first time Lily had called back, the other end of the line clicked to life at the precise moment she'd expected the sound of Nicole's voice-mail message. Yet Lily had been able to make out nothing but an odd muffled sound.

Talk about a bad connection.

The second time she'd called, the phone had clicked into voice mail after five rings.

Nicole must have already been on her way to her meeting.

The text message had arrived two hours later.

Lily sucked in a deep breath and powered on her phone, ignoring the fact she was in midflight and cell phones were supposed to be shut off and tucked away.

She accessed her saved messages and read the words for what had to be the hundredth time.

Sorry about tonight. Call you tomorrow.

But Nicole hadn't called her tomorrow. Instead, Lily had received a call from their parents, on their way home from the abbreviated anniversary trip.

Nicole had been found dead by a co-worker, murdered in cold blood.

Unease blossomed inside Lily's gut, spreading to her extremities.

According to police, at the time the text message had been sent, Nicole had most likely already been dead.

The lead detective on the case—she glanced at the name she'd jotted into her notebook—Cameron Hughes, was expecting her visit, no doubt itching to get his fingers on her phone.

If Nicole hadn't sent the message, who had? Her killer? And why?

Lily thought again of the sounds she'd heard during her first call back and her blood ran cold.

Had she heard her sister's struggle?

Lily shuddered as her plane bounced to a stop on the Philadelphia airport runway, and she braced herself. Braced herself for her impending meeting with Detective Hughes and for the sights and sounds of Nicole's funeral and her family's grief.

From the moment of her parents' call, shock had infiltrated her system like a wave of Novocaine, numbing her every sense and emotion. But as numb as she might be, Lily was certain of one thing. She wouldn't rest until Nicole's murderer had been brought to justice. Her true murderer.

A murderer proved by method, motive, opportunity and hard evidence.

Anything less would be merely adequate, and adequate wasn't good enough.

CAM AND HIS PARTNER, Vince Scarpello, headed back to the precinct, the images of what they'd seen hanging heavy between them. The medical examiner hadn't been finished with Nicole Christides's autopsy when they'd left, but they'd seen enough.

Within twenty-four hours they should have the cause of death, as if that weren't already obvious, as well as the time of death. Trace evidence hadn't yet yielded a thing, and Cam wasn't holding out too much hope.

"Someone went to the trouble of getting a big knife," Vince said flatly. "Convenient."

Cam nodded. "He's sticking to the familiar."

"Considerate of him."

Cam shook his head, knowing exactly what his partner was thinking. "He's smart enough to duplicate his earlier crimes to make us question whether or not someone else is taking advantage of his release."

"We still don't have a motive." Vince pursed his lips. "Maybe someone *is* taking advantage of Grey being out of jail."

Cam was doing a mental run through of the possibilities when they pushed through the precinct doors.

"You've got a Lily Christides waiting in interview three," the desk clerk called out as they stepped into the department office.

Cam and Vince nodded, neither saying a word until they were out of earshot.

"Consider this the first opportunity Grey's had to scratch his itch in over seven years." Cam shot Vince a look before his partner opened the interview-room door. "That's motive enough for me."

Cam stepped into an adjoining room, watching from the two-way mirror as Vince introduced himself to Lily Christides.

The woman might have spent the past five plus hours on a crowded airplane, but she was a knockout. Like her sister, hers was a classic beauty, yet the younger sister lacked the hard edge Nicole had perfected.

Grief and fatigue bracketed her dark eyes, but she remained standing even when Vince gestured for her to have a seat.

She reached into her purse, pulled out her cell phone and slid it across the table. Her long brown hair slipped over her shoulder, momentarily obscuring her soft features before she straightened, flipping the sleek length out of her face.

For a split second, she leveled her gaze to Cam's as if she could see him through the mirror. One corner of her mouth lifted before she refocused on Vince.

An odd sensation tightened Cam's gut but he ignored it, heading out of the observation room.

Ms. Christides was no dummy. She knew perfectly well someone stood watching her. He might as well join the party and watch her from his favorite vantage point when pursuing a case.

Up close and personal.

A few moments later all three sat around the interview table. Christides was well into the retelling of the story she'd told him over the phone.

She and her sister had spoken briefly then she'd attempted two callbacks.

"Tell me again about the reception on your first call back."

The woman patiently and professionally recounted what she'd heard. If Cam didn't know better, he'd think she had experience being on his side of the table. She related the facts without emotion.

Of course, her monotone voice was no doubt the shock talking.

"And then two hours later the text message came." She drew in a sharp breath and sat back in her chair.

Vince flipped open her cell phone and keyed in the necessary menu selections to pull up the saved message.

"Sorry about tonight. Call you tomorrow." Christides spoke the words without looking at the phone's screen, then she shook her head. "Obviously, she never called. My parents phoned me a few hours after that to let me know Nicole had been found dead, and I took the next plane out."

She flinched and Cam wondered if she might cry, but the woman caught herself. She straightened and breathed in and out slowly until she'd composed her features once more.

Stubborn, he thought. Stubborn and proud. Not an unattractive combination.

He reached for the phone, taking it from Vince's hand. "We'll need to keep this."

Christides nodded. "I'd imagined as much." She met his stare dead on, showing not a flicker of intimidation. "You'll verify the time of the message as well as the sender, correct?"

Too many crime scene shows, Cam thought as he nodded. "Exactly."

Vince pushed to his feet. "Let me get that started." He

extended a hand. "Ms. Christides, it was a pleasure to meet you. I'm sorry for your loss."

She nodded as Vince left, then her gaze locked with Cam's and held.

"Thanks for your time." He stood, but Lily Christides didn't move. She tipped up her chin defiantly.

"You like Grey for this, don't you?"

Cam shrugged. "Who wouldn't?"

"Anyone who has the intelligence to see my sister's murder as being a bit too convenient. The man was innocent of the prior charges."

"Three angry families would beg to differ."

"I take it you have difficulty believing an innocent man was convicted for those crimes?"

Disbelief and impatience raced through him. "And the guilty man held his cool for seven years? Didn't kill again until Grey was released from prison? Then killed the very person who helped overturn Grey's conviction?"

A moment of uncertainty played out across Christides's face. Even she had to admit the scenario he presented was more than a little implausible.

But instead of agreeing, she stood. "What if he's smart?"

"Grey?"

She shook her head. "Whoever killed my sister."

Cam thinned his lips. In his mind that person was Grey, and Christides knew it. "He is smart, Ms. Christides. Very smart."

He didn't voice the rest of his thoughts—that Nicole had probably brought about her own death by playing with the system simply to gain the spotlight.

She'd gained the spotlight, all right.

Front page on every paper in the country.

A week from now, people would barely remember Nicole's name. But Cam would. Cam would study her last days, her last hours, her last minutes. His mind would mull over her life and her death, not resting until her killer was back behind bars…this time for good.

LILY STARED AT DETECTIVE HUGHES and resisted the urge to grab the man and shake him. Honestly. Could he be any more obtuse when it came to her sister's case?

"So that's it?" she asked.

He stared without blinking.

"You've already zeroed in on your suspect?" she continued. "There hasn't yet been time for full autopsy results, am I right? How about the trace evidence report?" Lily ticked off the questions on her fingers.

"I know this guy," Hughes interrupted, his cool gray eyes staring at her as if she were off her rocker. He patted his chest. "I know you're angry and in shock, but leave the investigating to me."

Lily scowled and turned to leave, hearing her sister's final words in her head. *I'll call you back, Lil.*

And then reality hit her. There *had* been more.

Flowers.

She'd been reeling so hard from the news of Nicole's horrible death, she'd forgotten…until now.

She spun on one heel, hope flooding through her. "There were flowers."

Hughes frowned, his handsome brows drawing together. "Flowers?"

"Someone was at Nicole's door." Lily bit back her anger at herself. How could she have forgotten? "She said someone had brought her flowers."

Hughes shook his head. "There weren't any flowers at the scene."

"That's why she opened the door." Lily paced in a tight pattern. She jabbed a finger in Hughes's direction. "Your murderer used flowers to get her to open the door and then he took them when he was done."

The detective made no effort to hide his disbelief. "And you waited to tell me this until now?"

She rankled, frustration simmering deep in her gut. "I didn't remember before."

"You didn't remember the reason your sister opened the door?" A flush of impatience fired in his cheeks. "How do I know you aren't making this whole story up?"

This was going well so far. "And that would help my sister's case how? Detective Hughes, I am not an idiot."

"I never said you were."

"But you suggested…"

"I suggested nothing. I'm curious as to why you didn't share this information earlier."

Lily stepped close to where the detective stood, noticing the clean scent of whatever soap he'd used that morning. He frowned and tiny lines framed his intense eyes, his forehead puckering.

He should frown less, she thought, then shoved the wayward thought from her head.

"When was the last time you received a call telling you your sister had been brutally murdered?" Lily's voice cracked on the last word, and she winced at her show of weakness. "Much as it pains me to admit it, my brain isn't exactly firing on all cylinders."

"I don't have a sister," he answered, ignoring the second part of her statement completely.

Anger surged through her, sending heat flooding up her neck and face. Lily blinked, refusing to let the man's cold exterior faze her. "Then, do you have a heart?"

"That's debatable, Ms. Christides." He rested one hip on the table, folded his arms across his chest and met her stare. "That's debatable."

They stood in uncomfortable silence, neither one making a move to speak or turn away.

Hughes broke the silence first. "The Buddy Grey homicides were my first after I made detective." One corner of his mouth lifted. "I put him away once. I intend to put him away again. Whether or not you like him for your sister's murder isn't my concern. My only concern is the evidence, and the evidence is talking loud and clear."

Lily could see the conversation was going to get her nowhere. If she wanted a fair assessment of the facts in the case, she'd have to study them herself.

Hughes pulled a card from his pocket and thrust it toward her. He waited until she captured one edge between her fingers before he spoke. "If you remember anything else you may have forgotten, you can come to me, or I'll come to you."

Lily pulled a card from her purse. "The family business. They refuse to close and let their customers down, so I'm covering the evening shift. I'll be there until nine in case you decide to give me my phone back."

He took the card and met her gaze again, this time dropping his voice. "I'm sorry for your loss. Truly sorry."

A few moments later, Lily stepped through the precinct doors into the hot Philadelphia sunshine. She reached into her purse and flipped open her second cell phone, the one reserved for Body Hunters business.

She pressed a speed dial button and waited.

Rick Matthews answered on the first ring. "You all right?"

Was she all right? She was most definitely *not* all right, but she wasn't about to admit that to anyone, let alone one of the team's co-directors.

"I need you here," she said instead. "All of you."

Silence beat momentarily across the line.

Lily wasn't in the habit of admitting she needed help and Rick knew it.

"We'll be on the next plane out. I'll text you the safe house address as soon as I've made arrangements."

He disconnected and Lily snapped her phone shut.

Reaching out was just that simple, and yet reaching out was something Lily had never been much good at. Maybe there was a first for everything.

She unlocked her rental car, dropped into the driver's seat and keyed on the ignition. Then she headed toward her sister's address, drawn inexplicably by the need to see the spot where Nicole had breathed her last breath, spoken her last word, dreamed her last dream.

Soon, she'd be neck-deep in relatives and reporters and Body Hunters. Images of the first two sent chills through Lily's bones, but the last…the last provided more comfort than she ever thought possible.

Chapter Two

Lily pulled to the curb in front of Nicole's brownstone and cut the engine. Crime-scene tape blocked the entrance, pulled taut between the railings that edged the brick steps leading to the front door.

More than eighteen hours had passed since the approximate time of Nicole's death. Lily calculated the ticking clock without effort, her time with The Body Hunters having trained her to think in terms of hours and minutes while dealing with a murder investigation. The more time that passed, the less likely the authorities were to make an arrest.

She knew from experience the police wouldn't release the scene of the crime to the family until they were certain they had absolutely everything they needed.

Fair enough.

Lily reached for her computer bag and slid her laptop free of the straps that secured the padded compartment. Her wireless card instantly found the signal from Nicole's brownstone and Lily went to work. She opened the virtual storage site Nicole maintained for her work and investigations in progress, determined to find out who, if anyone, Nicole had been investigating who might want her silenced.

Lily didn't hesitate at the password prompt, confidently typing in the word *Savitch.*

Jessica Savitch, once a top female reporter in Philadelphia, had been Nicole's idol for as long as Lily could remember.

Lily's keystrokes were rewarded with entrance into Nicole's directory. Yet, the folder for stories in progress contained only one file. Notes regarding contact with a Gladys Sizemore.

Sizemore.

The name nagged at the back of Lily's mind, working to free some remembered fact she couldn't quite shake loose.

She tapped into The Body Hunters virtual private network, searching on the woman's name until she found what she hadn't been able to remember.

Tracey Sizemore had gone missing nineteen years earlier at a Poconos area summer camp. Gladys Sizemore, the girl's aunt and guardian, had worked ever since to keep the case alive in the minds of the public, media and law enforcement.

According to Nicole's notes, the woman had reached out following Nicole's media appearances in the Grey case.

Fourteen-year-old Tracey had vanished one day never to come home again. After months of searching with no leads, the local police had declared the case cold, filing away all evidence and case notes.

Could Nicole's interest in the story be tied to her murder? There was only one way to find out.

She pulled up the phone number for Gladys Sizemore and dialed, mentally crossing her fingers that the woman would be home. She was.

Five minutes later, Mrs. Sizemore reminisced about her

niece and recounted her conversations with Nicole. By the time they'd ended their call, Lily and Gladys Sizemore had a meeting set for ten o'clock the next morning.

Lily closed her cell phone, powered off her computer and accepted what her gut had known all along.

Her sister's murder had become the newest Body Hunters case—her sister's killer the next body to be found.

Soon the team would arrive in Philadelphia. They'd settle into the safe house, hold a body case briefing and go forward.

Rick Matthews would undoubtedly lead the way since Will Connor and his wife Maggie were traveling for the next month celebrating their second honeymoon.

Kyle Landenburg wouldn't miss the opportunity to work the case, Lily knew that. The quiet man had become one of her dearest friends, and she needed his wisdom and stability now more than ever.

Silvia Hellman would perform her computer magic while Martin Booker, the newest addition to the team, outfitted each operative with the latest and greatest in high-tech gadgets.

Lily smiled, feeling at home just envisioning the support she was about to receive.

She glanced at her watch, packed away her laptop and started the car's engine. She'd promised her parents she'd cover their dry cleaning shop tonight, and the last thing she wanted was for them to worry.

She'd catch up with her team later on.

Together, they'd work tirelessly until they brought the killer…and closure…home.

And this time, the family searching for justice would be like none Lily had faced on a single Body Hunters case.

This time, the family would be her own.

CAM REPLAYED HIS CONVERSATION with Lily Christides in his head, thinking of what little useful information the autopsy and crime-scene evidence had yielded.

Flowers.

Had there been flowers?

His team had checked every florist in the city—no small feat—and none showed any record of a delivery going to the dead reporter's house the night before. If there had been flowers, they'd been hand-delivered, but by whom? And from where?

There were over two-hundred-and-fifty florist shops in the city. Talk about your needle in a haystack.

The time of the text message and the tower that had received the signal matched Lily's story. Cam had also been able to confirm that Lily's outbound fifteen-second phone call with the lousy reception had in fact connected with Nicole's cell.

The reporter's phone had not been recovered from the crime scene, and its signal had not been picked up after the final text message.

Of particular interest was the fact the killer hadn't gone far from Nicole's brownstone before he sent the text, even though he'd waited for almost two hours. Matter of fact, the phone's signal had used the same tower used to serve Nicole's home.

Had Grey been that sure he'd go unnoticed? That sure he'd get away with what he'd done? Why?

Cam needed to question Lily about exactly what she'd heard over the phone. Could the noise have been her sister's fight for life?

A chill slid down his spine.

Even a tough son of a gun had to admit the emotional pain that knowledge would bring.

And of even more concern, what if the killer had realized the call connected? Realized the murder might have been overheard? Perhaps that explained why Nicole's phone had gone missing.

It didn't take a rocket scientist to read an incoming number, and Nicole no doubt had Lily in her contact list. Hell, the woman's name would have displayed for the killer's convenience.

An unwanted sense of protectiveness edged through him, and Cam reached for his pocket, grimacing at the feel of the pack of gum beneath his fingers.

He ran a search on Lily's name and background and came up with nothing of interest. Local girl makes good, relocates to Seattle and becomes a financial consulting whiz.

Something about Lily Christides called to him in a way no other woman ever had. The fire in her eyes. The challenge she presented, like a mystery waiting to be solved.

Cam's obsession with the Grey case had cost him everything he once loved. His wife. His young daughter. Hell, another man now lived with the family Cam had called his own once upon a time.

The only thing Cam took to bed each night were the images of those for whom life had been unfair, unkind, cruel. He owed them his full attention, and he'd given it—for seven years.

He raked a hand across his face and thought again of Lily's long dark hair, the soft lines of her face, the graceful way she moved and the way she seemed to see right through him.

He pulled his chair tight against the desk and reached for the business card she'd given him.

In case you decide to give my phone back. Her words bounced through his mind.

Chances were good she wouldn't be seeing her phone again any time soon, but he had directed the lab technician to download her phone numbers and personal photographs onto a disk.

Cam traced a finger across the card's embossed lettering. *Christides Clean and Fold.*

He tucked his cell phone into his pocket and stepped away from his desk. Now that he had new information and a copy of Lily's personal information, he'd be irresponsible if he didn't pay the young woman a visit.

He was still trying to convince himself that was his true reason for heading toward her parents' shop as he pushed out through the precinct doors into the warm summer night.

As Lily keyed in the security code to her parents' shop, fatigue screamed through her every muscle. She hadn't slept at all last night, and her nonstop activity had held off the crash of emotions until this moment. The reality of Nicole's murder had begun to take hold, but Lily fought to remain sharp and focused.

She was headed to meet The Body Hunters team to get their briefing under way.

A noise sounded not far behind her and she straightened, instantly shoving down all thoughts of grief and fatigue.

The nape of her neck tingled, a sure sign someone was watching her, but who?

Lily looped her purse over her shoulder, walking calmly toward the far lot where she'd parked her rental car. Afternoon parking in the city was notoriously difficult to find, and today had been no exception.

She cursed the distance silently. What she wouldn't give to be locked safely inside her car right now or walking on a crowded sidewalk.

This part of town boasted few restaurants and, as such, stood all but deserted this late on a Saturday night.

Footsteps sounded behind her, gaining fast. Her pulse quickened and the beat of her heart echoed the sound of heavy footfalls slapping against the concrete sidewalk, closing fast.

She squeezed her eyes shut, keeping up her pace, yet working to calm herself, even as she envisioned the person behind her. Closer now. Closer.

She dodged to her right at the moment of impact. A man's hand glanced off of her arm, making solid contact.

Was he trying to steal her purse?

Lily staggered, yet held steady. She couldn't afford to lose her balance or fall. She couldn't afford any move that might provide the man with the upper hand.

She studied the side of his face, but could see no distinguishing marks beneath the brim of his ball cap, pulled low and tipped down over his features.

The man was not out enjoying the city skyline, that much was certain.

She anticipated his next move—a sudden turn and attack—just as he made it, raising her arms defensively and planting her feet into a power stance.

Yet, as quickly as the man moved, a second man sprinted from the shadows.

Panic screamed to life inside her. Both figures were over six foot tall and solidly built.

Lily didn't stand a chance against a team of two.

The second charged and the first spun on his heel and

took off in a dead sprint. The second skidded to a stop, turning to study her. "Are you hurt?"

Stunned, Lily looked into Cameron Hughes's face and shook her head.

"Good." Cam tipped his chin toward her purse. "Check for your wallet."

"You think he was a pickpocket?"

One eyebrow quirked and he thinned his lips. "I'm thinking *no*."

Lily checked just the same. "Everything's there."

"Then he wanted to scare you—" he hesitated momentarily "—or worse."

"I think you scared him." Lily looked toward the empty expanse of sidewalk.

"Glad I was here."

Cam followed her gaze and Lily couldn't help but wonder at the mix of relief and suspicion battling inside her.

"Why are you here?" she asked.

"Had your numbers and photos downloaded from your phone to disk. Thought you might want them."

Lily blinked. She hadn't thought the man capable. "I didn't think you had a heart, Detective Hughes."

The shadow of a smile pulled at the corners of the man's mouth. "I believe those were your words, not mine."

His gaze met hers and held. Lily fought the urge to blink or look away. Attraction simmered between them and Lily worked to appear as unaffected as Cam seemed, even though the glimmer in his eyes hinted he might not be completely immune to the sensation.

She held out her hand, and his brows drew together.

"The disk?"

But instead of giving Lily her information, Hughes

pressed a palm to her back and steered her toward the still-lit entrance of a nearby coffee shop. "We need to talk."

THE MAN TOSSED THE BALL CAP into a trash receptacle as he headed back toward midtown. He couldn't risk the girl recognizing anything about him, even though there must be thousands of identical baseball caps in the city.

A thrill raced through him as he flashed back on the moment his arm had brushed against Lily's—a moment he would have enjoyed prolonging. Soon perhaps.

He laughed.

Of course, that depended on Lily Christides and what she had planned for the rest of her stay in the City of Brotherly Love.

He'd researched her, of course. Born and raised locally, she'd relocated to Seattle, leaving her parents and sister behind.

Had she heard his attack or his words when her call to Nicole's cell connected? The question had haunted him since the night before. He'd come here to see her for himself. To assess the enemy, so to speak.

The newspapers hadn't printed a word about any such evidence, but he wouldn't put it past the police department to keep that particular detail under wraps.

He'd also heard nothing about his text message. Fool. He'd never figured Nicole's body would have been found so quickly.

Oh well, the authorities would never trace the text message to him, so he wasn't worried.

What Lily Christides might have heard…that was a different matter.

If the woman had heard his voice, he'd deal with her.

Matter of fact, he'd arrange for her to spend an eternity of quality time with her dear, departed sister.

The Man laughed again, drawing frowns from a couple headed in the opposite direction on the quiet city sidewalk.

"Good evening," the couple spoke as one, obviously buying into the theory muggers wouldn't attack if you looked them in the eye and issued a greeting.

"It is, isn't it?" The Man replied, faintly annoyed they didn't recognize him.

He glanced down at his watch and grimaced.

If he didn't hurry, he'd be late for his first in person visit to Gladys Sizemore, and the last thing he wanted to do was keep the older woman waiting.

He'd initiated monthly phone calls four years ago, after she'd spoken to the media to mark the fifteenth anniversary of Tracey's disappearance. What better way to keep tabs on the woman and her activities.

He'd been disappointed to hear she'd reached out to Nicole.

So very, very disappointed.

Tonight, he planned to make sure Gladys Sizemore never reached out to anyone ever again.

Chapter Three

Body Clock: 27:15

Lily wrapped her arms around herself, hoping her trembling wasn't outwardly noticeable. She prided herself on not becoming rattled, but the thought of what might have happened if Cam hadn't rushed out of the shadows unnerved her.

She was trained to take care of herself, but truth be told, she would have preferred to skip the entire incident.

Cam phoned in a report and a description of Lily's would-be attacker. He'd been on the force for too long to think they'd actually catch the guy, or so he said.

"You think that was Grey?" she asked after the waiter poured two coffees and walked out of earshot.

Detective Hughes shrugged. "Build was right."

She snapped her tongue. "Build was right for half of the men in this city."

He blew out a breath and studied her. "Why are you so dead set against believing Buddy Grey killed your sister?"

"Let's just say I like to consider all angles."

"You learned that in finance school?"

Lily took a long sip of her coffee, savoring the soothing warmth. "You checked me out?"

The detective smiled. She hadn't thought it possible. "It's my job, Ms. Christides."

They drank their coffee, letting the silence stretch. "We verified the text message," Hughes finally said, breaking the quiet.

"From Nicole's phone?"

He nodded.

"It was sent after she was already dead?" Her stomach tightened on her last word.

Another nod. "Timing seems right."

"Why? To throw me off?"

"To throw everyone off, Ms. Christides."

She dropped her gaze to the tabletop, not wanting him to see how disturbed she was by what he'd said. Even though she'd expected as much, confirmation of the fact the killer had sent the text message was more unnerving than her speculation had been.

"There's more."

Lily lifted her gaze to meet the detective's. "What?" Her pulse quickened, thumping in her ears.

"Tell me again about the noises on the phone."

She blinked, the ramifications of his words hitting her like a freight train. "You think I heard *them?*"

Hughes didn't so much as blink. "The call connected. We believe you heard part of your sister's struggle, yes."

Lily put a hand to her mouth to block the bile clawing at the back of her throat. She braced her other hand flat against the tabletop and much to her surprise and dismay, Hughes gently placed his hand on top of hers.

"I'm sorry."

As quickly as he'd reached out to her, he withdrew his touch. His expression quickly morphed from concern to business. Lily wouldn't have believed the man capable of gentleness if she hadn't witnessed his actions with her own eyes.

"Did you hear anything recognizable during the call?"

Lily searched her memory, reliving the garbled seconds she'd attributed to a lousy connection. She'd heard muffled noise. Lots and lots of noise.

Tears blurred her vision and she blinked them away.

She shook her head.

"Nothing recognizable?" Hughes asked.

"Nothing."

Their gazes locked and for a moment Lily thought the detective might offer additional words of comfort. She was wrong.

"He didn't go far before he sent the text," Hughes continued, ignoring the fact she must be paler than pale. "The signal was picked up by the same tower as your calls received when Nicole was home."

Home being murdered, he should have said. "Meaning?" she asked.

"Meaning he's either staying nearby, or he went somewhere to kill time before he sent the text."

The detective's word choice left a lot to be desired. Lily straightened, working to gather her composure. "You're going to tell me you still think Grey's your man?"

Hughes nodded. "And your sister put him back on the street."

Lily had known the detective would voice that opinion sooner or later. It was more than apparent the man felt Nicole brought on her own death by freeing Grey.

She tamped down her anger and worked to keep her thoughts focused, not willing to give him the satisfaction of shaking her resolve.

"You think Grey is either staying locally or went somewhere to sit and wait? And no one recognized him?"

"We're canvassing the neighborhood as you and I speak."

She nodded, unsure about whether or not she should share her thoughts on the Sizemore case. "I found something in her files," she said, deciding the detective needed to know.

He frowned. "The house is still sealed off."

She read him instantly. He was afraid she'd set foot in his precious crime scene. "I pulled a name from her virtual network."

"Keep talking."

Lily took a long sip of coffee, a deep breath, then spoke. "I sat outside in my car and accessed her system."

"Anything you'd like to share?" His expression grew expectant.

"She was researching a new case."

"The station said she hadn't been assigned a new story."

Lily gave a quick lift and drop of her shoulders. "Doesn't mean she wasn't working on something."

"And?"

"Tracey Sizemore." She waited, wanting to see if the name rang a bell with the man.

"That was before my time," Hughes said slowly, his brow furrowed. "Teenager. Missing almost twenty years by now, I'd guess."

"Nineteen." Lily nodded appreciatively. "Good memory."

"It's my job, Ms. Christides."

"So you keep telling me."

His dark brows lifted toward his close-cropped hair. It

was nice to see peeks of the human beneath the detective every now and then. The glimpses gave Lily hope the man would bring her sister's true killer to justice no matter how dead set he was that Grey had committed the crime.

"You think she hit on something?" Hughes's question interrupted her mental tangent.

Lily nodded. "I'm meeting with Gladys Sizemore tomorrow at ten. She's the girl's aunt."

"Aunt?"

"Tracey Sizemore's parents died not long before she went missing. Gladys was her legal guardian."

Recognition of the name lit in the detective's eyes. "I've seen her on the news."

"Apparently she's never given up." Lily pushed to her feet. "Just like I won't give up, Detective."

She held out her hand and Hughes pulled a computer disk from his pocket, handing it to her. Lily tucked the object into her purse then turned to leave.

"Try to remember who the real investigators are before you head out on your wild-goose chase," he called after her.

Lily smiled to herself as she headed toward the exit door, reading the detective's warning loud and clear, but knowing exactly who the real investigators were.

The Body Hunters.

And she had no doubt they'd get their man—the correct man. No doubt at all.

CAM MAINTAINED A SAFE following distance as he trailed Lily out of Philadelphia and into the suburbs toward the Sizemore home the next morning. He'd gone back to work after he'd left her the night before, researching everything there was to find on the Tracey Sizemore disappearance.

It was bad enough he'd become distracted by the financial planner and her theory, but when he'd phoned the rural police department in charge of the Sizemore case nineteen years ago, the Providence Mills chief had told him evidence had gone missing years earlier.

Just like the victim, Cam thought, not liking the parallel.

Vince had stayed behind to continue the door-to-door questioning of neighbors and florists, determined to catch a break in the case. No one matching Buddy Grey's description had been seen at the local bus terminal or train station and, unless Grey had arranged for new papers, he hadn't taken a flight out of Philadelphia International. So where was he?

In the meantime, Cam set out to follow Lily. If the hot-headed beauty thought she was going to launch her own investigation at the possible expense of his case, she'd better think again.

This time, Buddy Grey was going down and going down hard.

And Cam planned to make sure nothing…and no one…got in his way.

He pulled his car to a stop along a tree-lined street, watching as Lily climbed from a rental car and walked quickly to the front door of a small ranch home. She moved with the grace and confidence of a martial arts trainee, not a financial planner.

A dancer perhaps, he wondered, then forced his thoughts away from Lily Christides, the woman, and back to Lily Christides, the victim's sister who was rapidly becoming a pain in the—

His thoughts broke off as Christides cupped her hand to the window next to the door, peering inside.

Perhaps Sizemore had changed her mind about the meeting. One thing was evident, Lily's knocking wasn't getting an answer.

She stepped away from the door and crossed to the garage, lifting onto her toes to peer inside. Hands fisted on her hips, she held her ground in the driveway momentarily before heading around to the back of the house.

Cam was out of the car and on foot in the blink of an eye. The last thing he needed was for some Nancy Drew wannabe to take up breaking and entering.

He spotted her the moment he rounded the back of the house. She expertly worked the doorknob, looking as if she picked locks for a living.

"You learn that in finance school?" he asked.

To his satisfaction, Christides gasped, dropping the small tool she'd cradled in her fingertips. "You followed me?" Her voice climbed indignantly.

Cam gave a sharp laugh. "I'd say I had good reason to, wouldn't you?" He moved quickly, closing his hand over the item she'd dropped before she could retrieve it.

He straightened, studying the set of expert lock picks. "They hand these out with your calculators?"

The woman glared at him. "I didn't get an answer."

Cam pursed his lips, working to keep his temper in check. "So you decided to slink around the back of the house and break in?"

Lily said nothing. Instead, she reached for the door, now ajar, and knocked one more time.

Silence.

"She was excited to see me, Detective. Something's wrong."

Cam stepped between Lily and the door. "Mrs. Sizemore. Hello?"

Nothing.

He eased the door open, moving slowly and methodically. An acrid smell hit him full force.

Something had been burning.

"Stay here."

Cam moved quickly through the utility room and kitchen then into a center hallway. One door stood closed and he knocked as he pushed it open to check the interior. A small bedroom. Empty.

He heard Lily's footfalls behind him as he headed toward the front of the house. "I thought I told you to stay outside."

But Lily never answered him, and he never repeated the question.

Instead, he pulled to an abrupt stop as he crossed the threshold into the home's living room. He turned quickly to block Lily's progress, but her eyes had already gone huge. She'd spotted the same thing he had.

"Don't touch anything," he said softly. "You all right?"

She nodded vacantly as he turned and headed toward the sprawled body in front of the fireplace. He checked for a pulse, but found none.

A single charred photo sat at the woman's fingertips, as if she'd plucked it from the flames, trying to save the image. The fireplace looked as though someone had tossed a pile of folders and photos inside and lit a match. A pill bottle sat on an end table next to a chair, upended and empty.

"Dead?" Lily asked.

"Very," Cam answered. Rubbing a hand across his face, he pulled his cell phone from his belt. As he made the call he realized he and Lily finally had something on which they'd no doubt agree.

Gladys Sizemore wasn't going to be answering any questions today. Matter of fact, she wasn't going to be answering questions ever again.

Chapter Four

Lily stood back as the argument between Cam and the local investigation unit heated up.

Over two hours had passed since they'd discovered Gladys Sizemore's body, and the number of officers on the scene had just taken a sharp drop.

"What do you mean you're done processing the scene?" The anger in Cam's voice strengthened Lily's resolve to get to the bottom of exactly what had happened.

The man might be a bit tough to take, but he took his job seriously. She had to give him credit for that.

His partner, Vince, arrived, edging past the young officer at the door. He shot Lily a quick nod and a tight smile.

"You two are out of your jurisdiction." The detective in charge had gone so red in the face Lily thought he might become the next victim. "I don't know how you boys handle your work in the city, but out here we do things by the book."

"Which book might that be?"

Lily winced at the tone of Cam's question. He was obviously upset with what he perceived as a less-than-thorough processing of the scene, but he wasn't going to win over the other detective by being difficult.

"The book that says a widow living alone with an empty bottle of pain pills next to her chair typically means suicide."

The other detective smiled, a man who knew he was in charge no matter how much Cam didn't like the fact. "No forced entry. No sign of struggle." He ticked off the points on his fingers. "We've taken the basics from around her chair and around the fireplace, but other than that, this one's pretty cut-and-dried."

"You're telling me your team already has the evidence they need to make that determination?" Cam stepped away from the other man and gestured widely. "And are you also going to tell me she—" he jerked a thumb toward the black body bag holding Gladys Sizemore "—burned up years of articles and photos and notes then killed herself? You believe that?"

Vince placed a hand on Cam's shoulder, putting a visible lid on his partner's anger.

"My mother takes these pills," the responding detective said, holding up the evidence bag containing the empty bottle. "The refill date on these was last week. The bottle is empty. She took enough to kill a horse."

"What about the one photo she pulled from the fire?" Cam spread his hands wide. "Why pull one out if you'd already decided to burn everything?"

The other detective merely shook his head. "I'm not a psychologist, Detective."

"She and I had a meeting," Lily interjected. "She was excited to see me."

She'd explained her reason for being at the house when

the police had first arrived, but no one seemed to care that the victim had made plans for that morning.

"She obviously changed her mind."

The impatience in the other man's eyes momentarily stole Lily's breath, then it angered her. Much to her surprise, Cam rose to her defense before she could say a word. He stepped to her side protectively.

"She's Nicole Christides's sister." He jerked a thumb in her direction. "I assume you've heard of that case? They do have television out here in the burbs, don't they?"

The other man scowled.

"Her sister was working on a story involving this woman's niece and Ms. Christides—" he pointed to Lily "—was scheduled to discuss their conversations with Mrs. Sizemore." His expression grew menacing. "Doesn't the timing of this woman's death raise some kind of alarm in your mind?"

The other man's lips quirked. "You're going to tell me you let a civilian schedule a meeting with a possible witness in your case? No wonder that Grey fellow is out on the loose again."

The anger and frustration radiating off of Cam's body were more than palpable. They were lethal. Vince moved quickly to block his partner at the precise moment Cam took a step toward the local detective.

For several long seconds, silence hung over the scene. Even the remaining technicians stopped working, their attention riveted to the standoff between Cam and their lead man.

Lily cleared her throat. "For your information, Detective Hughes tailed me. I had no intention of sharing my plans with him, but he saw right through me." Even though she had shared her plans, thankfully. Otherwise, she would have been alone when she discovered Gladys Sizemore's lifeless body.

She stole a glance at Cam, who now stared at her, confusion evident in his eyes. Apparently he wasn't used to financial planners spinning stories to back him up.

The tension in the room eased and the lead detective shook his head.

"Look, this isn't the first scene like this one we've processed. The coroner will give us the cause of death and I'll give you a call. But I wouldn't be holding my breath if I were you. Mrs. Sizemore more than likely timed her suicide so that Ms. Christides would find her body. Maybe she was tired of life and decided this was a convenient time to check out."

"And the picture she pulled from the fire?" Lily asked.

The other man nodded toward a tech gathering evidence. "Sentimental value, I suppose. Tagged and bagged. Can't see a damned thing in it, though."

Lily met Cam's gaze. The look that passed between them might have been lost on everyone else in the room, but Lily read the meaning loud and clear. Neither were ready to accept the suicide theory, but even if Sizemore had taken her own life, she'd pulled the single photo from the fire for a reason.

Lily needed to know what that reason was.

Cam tipped his chin toward the tech then refocused on Lily. He wanted that picture as much as she did. But how would they get their hands on it?

The investigative team began packing up their gear, and the coroner's wagon pulled up out front.

Lily needed a diversion, and she needed it fast. But what?

And then it hit her.

What she was about to do flew smack in the face of every ounce of pride she possessed, but sometimes a girl had to do what a girl had to do.

CAM WATCHED THE ARRAY of emotions wash across Lily's face. He no doubt was not making the best impression on the woman, but then, he wasn't here to make a good impression. He was here to understand exactly what had happened to Gladys Sizemore and why. Even more importantly, he was here to make sure the Sizemore death had nothing to do with his search for Buddy Grey.

As sidetracked as he might seem by this morning's developments, his mind was still focused on one goal. Nailing Buddy Grey with no room for error.

Lily studied him, and Cam knew exactly what she was thinking. The cops on the scene had already decided Sizemore had committed suicide. Even if she had, he wanted that photograph. Apparently, so did Lily. It didn't take a rocket scientist to know Sizemore wouldn't have pulled it out of the fire without reason.

"May I?" he asked as he stepped toward the small pile of bagged evidence.

The scene tech glanced toward the detective in charge, who nodded. The subtle approval was all Cam needed.

He located the bag containing the charred photograph and looked in Lily's direction. She studied him as intently as he'd been studying the evidence.

Her pale skirt hugged her every curve and her tailored white shirt fit her buttoned-up style. Hell, even her long hair had been twisted up and anchored to the back of her head. For a split second he fantasized about what the put-together woman might look like undone, but he shoved that thought out of his brain as quickly as it had appeared.

Lily widened her gaze and Cam nodded. She pressed a hand to her throat, then dropped like a stone.

Cam fought not to reach for his pack of gum. This was her idea of a diversion?

No wonder the woman had chosen financial planning as a career over…well…anything else.

Much to his dismay and relief, however, every male in the room rushed to Lily's side, Vince included. Cam, however, held his ground, sliding the bag containing the photograph from the evidence collection. He tucked it into the inside pocket of his jacket.

"I'll get her some water," one voice called out.

"How about a pillow?" another asked.

"Should we call for back up?"

"I'm sure she's fine," Cam interrupted, stepping through the gathered crowd.

Lily's dark eyes fluttered open at the sound of his voice, and if he wasn't mistaken the glare she shot him had everything to do with being annoyed and little to do with feeling dizzy.

Vince helped her to a sitting position and she blushed. "I'm so embarrassed. I don't know what came over me."

"You've had a shock." Vince anchored one arm around her waist. "Think you can stand?"

Cam shook his head and turned away, scanning the rest of the living area, searching for anything that might be missing or out of place.

Darned if the local investigation team hadn't been correct. The room showed no sign of a struggle. No sign of foul play. No sign of a forced entry.

Had Gladys Sizemore committed suicide? Choosing last night to coincide with Lily's visit today?

The entire scenario made no sense.

"I'll just pop into the rest room to freshen up." Lily's voice wedged itself into Cam's thoughts.

He turned in time to see her head down the hall toward the back of the house. His gaze held a moment too long on the lone tendril of dark hair that had escaped her hairdo.

"Nice show of your humanity, as usual," Vince said under his breath.

Cam flashed the concealed evidence bag and Vince scowled.

"You two had that planned?"

"You could say that."

Disbelief slid across Vince's face. "When did you two decide to play on the same side?"

"When Sherlock Holmes here turned up to process the scene." Cam patted Vince's shoulder. "Noticed you were quick to respond there, buddy."

Vince frowned. "Can you blame me?"

Cam smiled as he stepped away. "No." And the truth was, he couldn't blame Vince if he had an interest in Lily. The woman was beautiful, smart and apparently afraid of nothing. A man would have to be dead inside not to notice her.

"We're just about through here," the lead detective announced. "If you'd check on Ms. Christides, we can get the scene locked down until the autopsy and tox screen come back."

Cam headed toward the back of the house.

"Lily?" He stepped into the narrow hallway, spotting the

bathroom door wide open. If she hadn't gone there, where had she gone?

"In here," she answered. "The bedroom."

The bedroom? Maybe her swoon hadn't been an act after all.

"There's something under the bed."

Cam followed the sound of her voice, finding Lily peering beneath the fringe of a well-loved bedspread. "What are you doing?"

His question was answered by a growl—a deep, menacing growl.

"Tell me that wasn't you." He dropped to her side, kneeling down to have a look for himself.

"He's scared," Lily said. "I heard him whimpering when I walked past. Chances are he saw exactly what happened."

Cam replayed the morning in his mind, then shook his head. "No. This door was shut when we got here. Why would she do that?"

"To spare him from watching her die?"

Cam looked around the room, surprised by what he found, or rather, what he didn't find. "No food. No water."

Lily shook her head. "That doesn't make sense." She looked up at Cam. "Unless she believed I'd find her body and take care of her dog."

"I still can't see her leaving him without water at least."

She spoke next in a singsong voice. "Come here, baby. We won't hurt you." She shot a look at Cam. "At least, I won't hurt you."

Cam shot her an annoyed look before he lifted the edge of the bed covering, meeting the glowing eyes of a small Jack Russell terrier, if he weren't mistaken.

"You hungry?" Cam asked.

The dog whined.

"Then you'd better stop whining and get a move on." Cam sat back on his heels, holding the spread high.

The dog scampered out then sat in the middle of the floor facing the two of them.

"How did you do that?" Lily asked.

"The trick to dogs is letting them know who's in charge."

"Or bribing them with food."

"There is that."

A short while later, Cam and Lily stood outside, watching the crime-scene technician secure the scene. An animal control officer had taken away Gladys Sizemore's dog with the promise to find him a new home.

Apparently the dog was Sizemore's only survivor unless Tracey was still alive somehow…somewhere.

"Think they'll miss it?" Lily tipped her chin toward Cam's jacket and the hidden evidence bag. "What happens if it yields something useful? No judge will ever allow that in court."

The last thing he needed was a lesson in handling evidence, especially from Nicole Christides's sister. He ignored her question. "Ready to go?"

"Very."

The note of sadness in Lily's voice struck a chord with Cam, much as he hated to admit it.

The years had hardened him to the job, to the cases, to the bodies. But seeing today's scene through Lily's eyes made the senselessness all the more real.

No matter how she'd died, Gladys Sizemore was gone. With her had gone whatever she'd wanted to tell Nicole and then Lily. Unless the photo held the key.

Lily's gaze widened. "What next?"

He hooked his hand through her arm, steering her away from the house and toward her car.

"I'll ask around. See if I can locate someone who can restore this photo. We need to know why she pulled this from the flames."

Lily stopped, turning to study him. Beneath her scrutiny, Cam felt something he hadn't felt in years. Unnerved.

"What if I know someone who might be able to help you out?" Her question shoved all thoughts about how the woman made him feel from Cam's mind.

"I'm listening."

"Are you willing to come with me? To keep an open mind?"

He narrowed his gaze, frowning. "Just what kind of help are you talking about, Ms. Christides?"

One half hour later, he had his answer, and it blew his mind.

Before him stood a team of four. Three men. One woman. And a room outfitted with equipment the likes of which Cam had never seen in any local crime or forensic lab.

"Just what kind of financial planning is it that you do?" he asked.

Lily laughed, and he decided right then and there that he liked the sound. A lot.

"Detective Cameron Hughes," Lily said, pointing to the group before him, "meet The Body Hunters."

The Body Hunters.

He'd heard the term once, a bit of an urban legend, a group whose existence had never been proved, but whose work had been mentioned in hushed tones in various law enforcement circles.

The group in front of him was anything but an urban

legend, and their determined expressions, diagrams and charts were as real as real got.

Lily introduced each member in turn.

Rick Matthews, co-founder of The Body Hunters and a trade-show producer in his public life.

Kyle Landenburg, a security expert as far as the public was concerned.

Silvia Hellman, a retired librarian and research expert.

Martin Booker, a technology whiz and computer programming genius.

"The Body Hunters," Cam said under his breath. "Well, I'll be damned."

Chapter Five

Body Clock: 42:40

The Body Hunters.

Cam frowned as he studied Lily. She was anything but what he would have pictured for someone part of The Body Hunters.

She smiled as if reading his thoughts.

That was the point, wasn't it? Most suspects would never see her coming. Young, beautiful, unassuming. She'd be a master at blending in and getting attention and results at the same time.

"I do believe we've left you speechless, Detective Hughes." Her face lit with delight and something deep inside Cam caught and twisted.

He had no time to be intrigued by Lily Christides. No time at all.

"You might as well call me Cam now that you've shared your secrets."

"Fair enough…Cam."

He quickly studied each member Lily had introduced.

He would have never expected Silvia and Martin to be anything but what they were in their "real" lives.

Kyle, on the other hand, looked every bit the role of Body Hunter. Matter of fact, with his military cut and intense features, he looked every bit of the hunted, not hunter.

Rick Matthews was another matter altogether. Polished and a bit aloof, the man left no room for wondering exactly who was in charge. He exuded control and confidence.

Cam scanned the faces once more, then took stock of the equipment covering every inch of available space.

He'd need to keep tabs on this group. Very, very close tabs.

Even if they remained focused on the Sizemore girl and not on Buddy Grey, they looked as though they knew just enough to be dangerous, and dangerous was something he couldn't afford. Not this time.

He'd played by the rules before and look how that had turned out. Maybe this time, he'd break a few. Hell, he'd already gotten a running start. He patted the pocket containing the evidence bag.

"We heard about Sizemore." Rick reached for Lily. "I'm sorry."

Lily forced a bright expression. "I may not have gotten to speak with the poor woman, but we did take a piece of evidence with us."

Kyle's eyebrows lifted, as did Rick's.

"Evidence?" Silvia asked. "You don't like the suicide theory."

Lily's features twisted. "Something doesn't seem right, no. And she'd pulled a photo from the fireplace." She caught herself, visibly retracing her mental steps. "Apparently she'd burned everything she'd saved regarding her niece's disappearance."

The older woman blinked. "Burned them?"

"Everything but this." Cam pulled the bag from his pocket.

Each pair of eyes in the room watched as he set the bag on a desktop.

"And that is?" Rick asked.

"A charred photograph," Lily answered. "The one Mrs. Sizemore pulled from the fire."

"Like she'd changed her mind?" Silvia asked.

"Or like she hadn't wanted someone else to get away with destroying it."

With Cam's words a hush fell across the room.

"How did you manage to lift it?" Rick tipped his chin toward the bag.

"I fainted." Lily shrugged.

"Fainted?" Silvia's voice climbed several octaves as she hastened to her feet.

Kyle's eyes narrowed suspiciously, yet he eyed Cam, not Lily, as if somehow Cam were responsible for what had happened. Something rankled to life in Cam's gut. He thought it jealousy, but that would be insane.

"I was pretending," Lily continued, refocusing the group's collective attention. "I needed to cause a diversion."

"And that was the best you could do?" Rick Matthews's lips curved into a grin.

"It worked." Lily straightened.

"You approved of this?" Rick directed his question at Cam.

Cam nodded. "The only place that crew was going to put this photo was into an evidence box."

"He's right." Lily lifted the bag from the desk, crossed to where Silvia sat, and gingerly handed her the object. "Can you do anything with this?"

"I can." Martin spoke without giving Silvia a chance to respond. "We can use the same technology used in age progression to restore the features based on the structure remaining in the picture itself."

Much to Cam's surprise, Silvia smiled proudly. "My thoughts exactly."

LILY WATCHED THE SURPRISE play out on Cam's face.

The detective apparently wasn't used to true teamwork. Well, if he stuck around, he'd find out what teamwork really meant.

"We'll start by scanning a copy of the original so that we have something a bit less fragile to work with," Martin continued.

"How will you capture the fine details?" Cam asked, visibly intrigued.

"Watch and see." The young man's features brightened as he worked, handling the photo with padded-tipped tweezers, positioning the height setting on a scanner a few inches above the charred paper.

"How did you get all of this equipment here?" Cam asked.

"It's our job," Lily said.

Cam met her gaze and smiled. The taunt hadn't been lost on him. Perhaps there was hope for the detective yet.

She smiled, enjoying the moment until she remembered exactly what had brought this particular group of people together this time.

Her sister's murder.

Nicole. Gone forever.

Emotion choked Lily and she looked at her feet as Martin continued to explain each step of the reproduction process.

"You okay?"

Typically, Lily would have expected to find Kyle by her side asking the concerned question, but much to her dismay it was Cam who had closed the space between them and now gripped her elbow.

His cool gaze searched her face, as if he'd never truly seen her before. For one crazy moment, Lily longed to lean into him, longed to tuck her face into his neck and let loose the tears threatening just beneath the surface of her control.

But just as quickly as she'd entertained the ridiculous fantasy, she shoved it away.

Cam Hughes and she differed on one vital point.

In his eyes, Nicole had knowingly freed a murderer. Lily refused to fall for anyone who thought her sister capable of doing such a thing.

Lily pulled her elbow from Cam's fingertips and took a sideways step. "I'm fine."

"Problem?" A second deep voice sounded, this one Kyle.

He shot Cam a warning glance then hooked one arm around Lily's shoulders. She let down her guard long enough to lean into the man who'd become the big brother she'd never had.

"Everything's good," she answered, her gaze locking with Cam's one last time. "No problem at all."

But as the detective turned away, her body betrayed her, suddenly craving his touch. His nearness. His voice.

Her grief was obviously wreaking havoc on her emotions. She needed to pull herself together…but quick.

CAM STEPPED AWAY FROM LILY, moving closer to where Martin and the team focused.

Lily apparently had found all the comfort she needed in the form of Kyle Landenburg.

An odd wave of emotion washed through Cam's system. Protectiveness. Jealousy. Attraction.

All emotions for which he had no time, nor inclination.

Seeing Lily sink into the embrace of the big man was exactly what Cam needed to snap himself back into focus.

Good riddance.

He'd use her to keep an eye on the rest of The Body Hunters team, nothing more.

What he needed now was to get in touch with Vince. The medical examiner's final report on Nicole should be complete by now. Then Cam would bite back his pride and apologize to the investigative team on the Gladys Sizemore case.

Cam had acted like a jerk and he knew it. Plus he needed access to the results of the investigation. He had to make sure the Sizemore suicide was in no way related to the Christides murder.

He wouldn't be a detective if he didn't question the timing of both deaths and the fact the women had talked and met within the past few weeks.

Coincidences did happen, yes, but he'd never been a fan of the phenomenon.

"And there you go." Martin Booker's voice interrupted Cam's thoughts.

The photo had been reproduced, larger than life on a flat-paneled computer monitor. The damage was no less evident, yet the surviving detail was intensified, clarified somehow by the resolution of the scan, the screen size and the sharpness of the display.

"Amazing." Cam blew out a whistle. "And now you'll work to restore it?"

Martin nodded. "The program will work section by section to blend and restore. The process takes days, I have to warn you, but the results are typically mind-blowing."

Mind-blowing.

As if Cam hadn't already had enough mind-blowing developments in his career during recent weeks, starting with the Grey conviction falling to pieces.

He raised a brow as Martin slid the original photo back into the evidence bag. "With any luck at all, you can return this before they realize it's missing."

"You won't need it again?"

The young man beamed. "The copy I just made is a better original than the original, trust me."

Cam and Rick exchanged contact numbers, and Rick promised to call as soon as the photo produced a usable image.

Cam's mind raced as he headed back outside to his car. With any luck at all, returning the photo would go off without a hitch and he'd be able to tap into the information stream coming out of the Sizemore investigation.

At the same time, the task gave him the perfect opportunity to put some space between him and Lily Christides.

The woman's presence had begun to cloud his thoughts, and that was something to which he wasn't accustomed. It was also something in which he had no interest.

Her face flashed across his mind's eye and he fisted his hand, remembering the feel of her slender arm beneath his touch.

He had no interest in Lily Christides as anything other than a means to an end.

And if he kept telling himself that, he just might believe it.

"Do you think he's going to be a problem?" Rick asked the second Cam pulled away from the curb outside.

"Could be." Lily stared at the empty space where Cam's car had sat parked moments earlier. As a rule, the team was usually more cautious about bringing someone from the outside world into their confidence, but she needed the photo, and her gut told her Cam could be trusted. "He's not a fan of the private investigative group concept, that's for sure."

"I think the term he'd use would be *rogue*." Rick smiled.

"Speaking of rogue—" Lily turned away from the window and stepped back toward the war room "—what do we have on Nicole's case?"

When she and Cam had walked into the house and then into the war room, Lily had been more than relieved to find no trace of The Body Hunters's investigation into Nicole's death.

The team had decided to run both investigations simultaneously, agreeing there was a high likelihood the murders were somehow connected, if for no reason other than that Nicole had spoken with Sizemore on more than one occasion during the past few weeks.

The team waited downstairs, ready to go, as if Cam had never set foot inside the safe house.

Silvia passed out a printed list of bullet points—the Body Case, as they called the official briefing at the start of an investigation.

"Thank you all." Lily said the words quickly and without elaboration. Silvia, Kyle, Martin and Rick all gave her tight nods, knowing how deep the words went.

"Now then—" Rick pulled out a chair as he headed toward the wall now covered in flowcharts, head shots and maps "—let's get this show on the road."

"According to phone records—" Silvia spoke first, referring to a printout she clutched in her hand "—Nicole made three calls to Gladys Sizemore in the week before her death. She also made numerous calls to city hall."

"Tim's office?" Lily asked, referring to Tim Fitzsimmons, executive director of Rebuild Philadelphia, Nicole's most recent romantic interest.

"Apparently not." Silvia pursed her lips. "These all went to the mayor's office." She corrected herself, waving a finger. "No, no, specifically the Office of External Affairs."

"Ross Patterson," Lily interjected. "The heir apparent."

The incumbent mayor had decided not to seek reelection. His right-hand man, Patterson, had accepted the party nomination and was expected to win the general election that fall.

"Exactly." Silvia shot Lily a proud smile. "I thought you were a full-fledged Seattle girl now, but you know your native city."

"Trust me, my sister and my parents keep me informed."

My sister.

A heaviness descended, but Lily forced herself to focus through the mental fog that had permeated her brain over the past two days.

"Thoughts on why Nicole would have been calling Patterson's office?" Rick asked.

"Maybe he was connected to a new story she was working on." Kyle spoke the statement flatly and Lily recognized his tone of voice.

The man had certain intuitive abilities that no one ever mentioned, but everyone on the team accepted. Thoughts and visions came to him, in direct opposition to his hardened exterior—the military haircut, the silent demeanor.

When Kyle did speak, the rest of The Body Hunters knew to take him seriously.

Rick pointed to Lily. "What other new stories did you find in Nicole's virtual files?"

Lily shook her head. "None."

The group grew quiet, and hard as Lily worked to make her brain address the puzzle before them, her mind wouldn't cooperate.

Instead she pictured Gladys Sizemore, dead on the floor, the photo at the tips of her outstretched fingers. She pictured the dog, frightened and hiding beneath a bed. She pictured what appeared to be years of notes and memories tossed into a fire.

Then she pictured Nicole, laughing, reporting, living.

Emotion squeezed at her throat, choking her. She dropped her focus to her hands, clasped so tightly together in her lap her knuckles had gone white.

"Lily?" Kyle's voice.

A hand on her shoulder. A kind face. Silvia's.

"I'm okay." She forced a smile. The team's grim expressions suggested no one believed her. "How about Grey? Any word on him? Movement? Sightings? Family?"

Martin spoke this time. "He's either operating using cash or using an assumed identity."

"Would he have had time to acquire new identification or cash?" Lily asked.

Martin grinned, his enthusiasm for the chase as fresh as it had been the day he joined the team. "We outsiders fail to realize what a separate world prison is, or how fully formed that society is. I'm sure he could have had anything waiting for him on the outside. The trick now is to break whatever cover he's using."

"What about family?" Kyle asked.

"Mother," Kyle answered. "Dorothy Grey. Still resides in the house where Buddy Grey and his brother grew up."

"Brother?" Lily could barely believe her ears.

"Apparently he went missing nineteen years ago." If Kyle saw the significance of the timing, he didn't let on. Of course, Kyle prided himself on never showing what he was feeling.

Lily zeroed in on his words. "The same year Tracey Sizemore went missing?"

Silvia gave a sharp nod. "The same."

"How long after did the killings start?" Lily pushed to her feet.

"I know what you're thinking," Silvia continued. "The original killer couldn't have been the brother. The DNA was a spot-on match. So spot-on, in fact, it almost appears too good to be true."

Silvia shrugged before she continued. "Too close for siblings, regardless." She held up a finger as if catching her thoughts. "Unless they're identical."

Kyle shook his head. "Three-year age difference."

"Where's the mother?" Lily asked.

"Portland, New York."

"How—"

"Seven to eight hours," Kyle answered without waiting for the rest of Lily's question. "Fairly direct from here to there."

Lily's gaze moved past Silvia to the worktable behind her. Several squares and triangles of cotton cloth sat positioned into a pattern. Lily recognized the significance instantly. A quilt in the making—Silvia's method of release during a case.

Whenever someone went missing, the older woman made a quilt—a labor of love—for the victim.

Yet in a case such as Nicole's, the quilt would be offered to the survivors, a tangible comfort to cling to in moments of grief and healing.

Lily squeezed her eyes shut momentarily. The image of Nicole burned into the back of her lids, followed in quick succession by the image of her lying dead on a coroner's slab, then lifeless in a coffin.

Lily rubbed her face and shook away the unwanted images, accurate or not.

"Has the mother been interviewed?" she asked absently.

"According to my contact inside the police department, routine questioning hasn't turned up a thing," Rick said. "The only thing Dorothy Grey has said is that Buddy is innocent on all counts."

Rick's features tensed, and Lily realized he'd read the grief on her face.

"Anyone mind if we go over this a bit later?" She voiced the question before she was forced to endure the embarrassment of being told to walk away for a bit.

No one said a word, and Lily didn't think twice about the silence. They knew her well enough to know she was the first person to work around the clock on a case, doing whatever it took to bring home a missing child, a missing spouse, a wanted criminal. But today...today she hurt too much to wrap her brain around any additional information.

She headed for the room she'd taken in the safe house. She'd chosen to stay here in order to be in the middle of the investigation, yet she had to admit she wouldn't mind curling up in a ball on her parents' sofa right about now.

She'd told her parents she was staying in a local hotel in order to give them space for other out-of-town relatives. They'd told her they understood, but Lily knew they hadn't, not fully. How could they? They knew nothing about her role in The Body Hunters.

Lily had spoken to her father on her way to the Sizemore house that morning. Nicole's body had been released to the funeral home as promised, and the services scheduled for the next afternoon had been confirmed.

Every time Lily thought about seeing the casket, knowing her sister lay dead inside the steel walls…well…she felt weak, and weak was something Lily had fought her whole life.

When she reached the solitude of her room, Lily changed into a pair of jeans and a cotton T-shirt, took the clip out of her hair and slipped her feet into her favorite sneakers.

She sank onto the edge of the bed, admiring the serene decor of the room. Taupe, burgundy, antique-white. She'd think the space lovely if she were here for any reason other than working to track her sister's killer.

Lily pushed to her feet, needing air, needing distance.

She drove on instinct, visiting the memories of her childhood, the memories of Nicole.

When the afternoon shadows began to grow long, she came to terms with the fact she could never bring her sister back. It was too late to save Nicole.

But it wasn't too late to save someone else.

She headed for the animal shelter, navigating the city streets as if she'd never moved away.

Turned out Prince, the Jack Russell terrier, had been cleared for adoption. His vaccinations and name had been vouched for by the veterinarian whose standard-issue rabies tag hung from the dog's collar.

"If you're unsure, you could always foster him until

someone else shows an interest." The shelter's manager on duty tapped a pen against his clipboard.

And then say goodbye to someone else in her life? Lily thought as she stood at the dog's cage.

No thanks.

She studied the terrier's eager expression, and realized she'd made up her mind the moment she'd left the safe house.

"I'd like to adopt him, please."

Thirty minutes later, Prince sat on the front passenger seat of her rental car, calm and collected, even though he must be wondering what had happened to his safe, secure world.

Lily knew exactly how he felt.

Her cell phone rang and she pulled to the side of the road before answering. She'd never been someone who could talk and drive at the same time. Chalk it up to her preference for fully focusing on one task at a time.

Rick launched into conversation without offering a greeting. "Hughes called looking for you. He's at the precinct."

Lily was about to ask why when she caught herself. Rick didn't like stupid questions and asking him what Hughes wanted would definitely fall into that category. She needed to track down Hughes for herself.

She mentally chastised herself. Yes, she was brain-deep in grief, but she had to focus. Had to hold herself together. Nicole's case depended on it.

"Where are you?" Rick asked, apparently concerned by the silence on her end of the line.

Lily reached over to scratch the Jack Russell terrier behind the ears. "Just left the pound."

"Visiting Sizemore's dog?" Rick's tone shifted to one of suspicion.

"You could say that."

She'd mentioned the dog only briefly back at the house. She should have known Rick would remember. The man remembered everything.

"Is he sitting next to you in the car?" This time, Rick's voice gave away his smile.

Lily grinned. "You could say that, too."

Her co-director's rich laughter rumbled across the line. "Check in and let me know what Hughes wants, when you can."

"Will do."

She disconnected and blew out a deep sigh. The dog tipped his head to one side, then whimpered. Lily stroked his muzzle and he leaned into her touch. "Sorry for your loss, buddy. We're going to find out what happened, don't you worry."

A split second later, she was back on the road, refocused on heading straight toward the precinct and whatever burning questions Cam Hughes had ready for her.

Chapter Six

Body Clock: 47:20

Reporters and news vans swarmed the precinct as Lily approached. She instinctively drove past, pulling into a restaurant parking lot to call Cam.

"What's going on?" she asked as soon as he answered.

"And hello to you, too."

She smiled in spite of herself. The man was just infuriatingly arrogant enough to be likable. Go figure. "I got your message."

"Where are you?"

"Down the block. I didn't want to get trampled by the media."

"Drive around the back and pick me up."

"Did you want to add anything to that request?" She issued the challenge even as she restarted the ignition.

"Now."

The phone clicked in her ear and she blew out a sigh. The man was unbelievable.

A moment later, Cam stood at the passenger door, glowering at the dog. "You didn't."

"I did." Lily pulled herself taller in the seat.

Cam snapped his fingers. "In the back, dog."

The terrier launched himself out of the front seat and into the back, climbing to look out a window, bracing his front paws against the door.

"Hope you got the extra insurance," Cam said as he dropped into the rental car.

"Why do you have such a chip on your shoulder?" Lily had always been one to speak her mind. She could see no reason why dealing with Cam Hughes should be any different.

He patted the chest pocket of his jacket and swore. "Because victims' relatives won't let me do my job."

"Hey—" Lily pulled away from the back entrance "—*you* called me. What's up with the press?"

"Autopsy report came back. I wanted to fill you in."

Autopsy report.

Cold slabs. Coroner's tools. Lily swallowed down the knot in her throat and told herself to be strong.

She'd known this was coming. Once Nicole's body had been released, the medical examiner's report couldn't be far behind.

Unwanted mental images assaulted her just the same.

She forced herself to focus on Cam. On driving. On anything but the thoughts of Nicole's battered body.

Perhaps seeing her sister's crime-scene photos would have been preferable to the pictures her imagination had conjured up.

Lily shoved the thought away. Those images were ones she never wanted to see.

"Where to?" She forced the words through her lips.

When Cam answered, the surprise of what he said over-shadowed every image of death and loss in Lily's brain.

LILY'S APPEARANCE HAD STOLEN Cam's breath away when he'd first climbed into her car.

A pair of faded jeans hugged her curves, topped by a plain white T-shirt. She'd loosened her hair, and rich brown waves fell down her back. The sight of her undone surprised him.

Yet, the fact he'd told Lily to drive to his brownstone surprised Cam even more. If he weren't careful, he'd cross the mental line between professional and personal—a line he had no intention of crossing. A line he couldn't afford to ignore if he wanted to remain objective on the case.

He studied his living area through her eyes as they stepped through the door, realizing how stark and cold the space had become.

Become actually wasn't the right word. More like *remained.*

He'd never decorated. Never painted.

The walls remained the same neutral color they'd been the day Cam moved in. The hardwood floors remained less than gleaming. His furniture remained as utilitarian and functional as it had been before his decision to invest in one of the city's up-and-coming neighborhoods.

The one bright spot of the home was the collection of vivid crayon drawings he'd framed and hung on the living room's brick walls.

Lily lifted her brows in question, not voicing her curiosity.

Cam offered a single word response. "Daughter."

The blatant surprise on Lily's face rocked him. Had he become so callous that the thought of him fathering a child was unthinkable?

His stomach grumbled and he realized he'd eaten nothing since he'd fried up eggs that morning. The same could probably be said for Lily.

"Hungry?"

If possible, the woman's eyes widened even further. "You cook?"

"A man's got to eat."

The Jack Russell terrier scampered into the kitchen, assumed a sitting position and whined.

"Apparently so does a dog," Lily observed.

Cam grabbed a cereal bowl from a kitchen cabinet, filled it with cool water and set it in a corner for the terrier, who greedily lapped up the contents.

"I have some leftover chicken." Cam studied the contents of his mostly empty fridge. "Sound all right?"

Lily nodded and he once again noticed how hard she was working to hide her fatigue and grief. He remembered how shell-shocked he'd been in the days after his wife had moved out without warning, taking their daughter.

Just the memory of walking into their home and finding it stripped bare pulled at him, squeezing at his chest.

He couldn't begin to imagine what Lily must be feeling, but after years of dealing with grieving relatives, he knew the worst was yet to come. At this point, she was still largely operating on shock and adrenaline.

He pulled back a curtain to reveal a set of French doors that opened to a patio. A bistro table and chairs sat on the stone patio, and a half-dead plant claimed the center of the table.

"I probably should water that once and a while. Make yourself at home."

He sliced up some leftover chicken, layering the pieces with fresh tomato, mozzarella and salad greens.

He'd learned over the years that in order to survive, he needed a basic level of skill in the kitchen. He filled a bowl for the dog and grinned as the terrier inhaled the chicken.

Lily stood at the table outside, absently picking at the plant. When she stepped back into the kitchen, pot in hand, the plant resembled an actual living thing.

"She just needed some attention." She stood next to him by the sink. "May I?"

Cam opened the spigot and she moistened the plant's soil.

"Miracle worker." He tipped his chin toward the pot.

Their gazes met and held, and moisture shimmered in Lily's eyes. "For some things."

"We'll get justice for your sister." Cam grasped her shoulder and squeezed. "I promise."

He dropped his hand, but the moment held between them as if suspended in time, until Lily blinked, then turned away. "Thanks for feeding me. And Prince."

Cam grimaced. "Hell of a thing to name a dog."

"What's wrong with it?"

The dog danced around Cam's feet as he carried their salads out to the table.

Cam frowned. "Please. He deserves something more appropriate. Something that fits his personality."

"You've known the dog for a matter of hours. Are you going to tell me you've analyzed his personality?"

Cam nodded. "I recognize his type." He maintained his standard unemotional tone of voice, but even Cam had to admit the dog's spunk and personality were growing on him. Having Lily and the dog in Cam's house made it feel more like…a home.

Lily pulled out a chair, sat down then crossed her arms.

"And what type is that?" A smile tugged at the corners of her full lips. "This I want to hear."

Cam dropped to one knee, scratched the dog's head and made a show of studying the terrier's face. "Trouble." The Jack Russell terrier catapulted into Cam's arms and licked his chin.

Lily laughed softly and rolled her eyes. "Men."

Cam did his best to ignore the way his body responded, the way his gut tightened with the sudden desire to pull her into his arms and tell her everything would be all right again. Someday.

"You were going to tell me about the report?" All trace of laughter left her face.

Lily's question shattered the mood and the moment was lost.

Cam straightened, studying Lily's expectant, yet tentative, expression.

But before he could say a word, something crashed inside the house. Tires squealed out front and an explosion rocked the very ground on which Cam stood.

He dove for Lily, knocking her from her chair and onto the stone patio. He covered her body with his, working to comprehend what was happening as adrenaline surged through his veins.

When the second explosion came, heat and flames flared above them.

Dinner and news of Nicole's autopsy report had become the furthest thing from Cam's mind.

First and foremost were two things.

Saving Lily's life, and getting the two of them the hell out of harm's way.

Chapter Seven

Cam did his best to shield Lily's body with his own. The force of the explosion left his ears ringing and his senses stunned. Flames licked at the interior of the house and, from somewhere inside, more glass shattered.

"What happened?" Lily asked, her voice frantic.

He studied the twelve-foot wrought iron fence that surrounded his small piece of concrete. The only way out was through the alley that ran alongside the house.

More breaking glass.

They had to hurry.

Lily followed his glance to the fence then to the alley. She nodded her understanding.

"Now." He gripped her hand and pulled her to her feet.

Heat pushed at his face and black smoke swirled into the small yard that had moments ago been the scene of their almost-shared meal.

"Where's the dog?"

Panic shone in Lily's eyes.

Cam quickly scanned the yard, but the dog was nowhere in sight. "He's gone. He'll show up. Don't worry."

"We can't leave him." She raised her voice above the sound of the flames waging war on what had been Cam's life, such that it was.

He pulled at her, anchoring an arm protectively around her waist as he moved her into position to run for the front gate. "We have to," he said just as the wail of sirens sounded in the distance, drawing closer.

"What if he ran back inside?"

What if the dog *had* run back inside?

Another explosion of glass sounded, and something boomed, sounding suspiciously like part of the floor giving way.

If the terrier had run back inside, he'd never survive, but Cam had to get Lily to safety before he could worry about the dog.

"We have to go. Now." He urged Lily forward.

This time she didn't argue.

They moved as one, Cam between Lily and the inferno of his home, Lily pressed close to the fence. They ran without looking back until they emerged onto the street, relatively unscathed.

If they'd been inside at the time of the explosion—

Cam censored his own thoughts. He wasn't about to let his mind explore the possibility of what that outcome might have been.

Lily's brows drew together and moisture glistened in her eyes.

The dog.

She'd never forgive Cam if he didn't go back for the dog. He gave her hand a squeeze, then raced toward the alley, only to find himself intercepted by Vince.

"I came as soon as the address hit the wire."

Cam pushed at his partner, trying to free himself of the other man's embrace.

"Where in the hell are you going?" Vince asked.

Cam didn't have time for a full explanation. "There's a dog. It's complicated."

Flames burst through a second-floor window, sending a shower of glass to the sidewalk below.

Cam and Vince hit the pavement, covering their heads with their arms. Cam tried to scramble to his feet once the immediate threat passed, but Vince grasped his upper arm, holding firm.

"If there was a dog inside that house, he's gone, man. I'm sorry. You can't go back in there. You know I'm right."

Vince *was* right. Truth was, Cam knew he was already too late even before the inferno pushed him back. But he'd wanted to be able to try.

He grimaced, angry at himself for not moving faster, mad at the dog for taking off, and furious at whoever had destroyed his home.

"What happened?" Concern tightened Vince's features.

Several firefighters sprang into action, racing into position.

"I think someone hurled a firebomb through my front window." Cam pushed to his feet, walking backward, out of the firefighters' way, never taking his eyes from the blaze. "And I intend to find out exactly who that someone was."

HOURS LATER, A LONE FIRE CREW remained at the brownstone, hosing down the smoldering shell.

The arson investigator had come and gone with the promise to phone Cam as soon as he had definitive word on the materials used in the attack. Vince had headed back to the station after making Cam promise to put Vince's spare bedroom to use until he could get back on his feet.

"I need to get you out of here." Cam walked toward where Lily sat perched on the hood of her rental car.

A bark sounded and Lily straightened beside him. "Did you hear—"

Another bark. This one closer. Stronger.

The brown-and-white blur raced down the sidewalk, moving so fast Cam thought for a moment the dog might be a wishful figment of his imagination.

"Trouble." The name on Lily's lips was music to Cam's ears.

She dropped to her knees and the dog launched himself into her arms, slurping at the happy tears that slid down her face.

Lily gave the dog a squeeze, shot a smile at Cam, then returned her full attention to the terrier. "I'll never let you out of my sight again."

That's funny, Cam thought. That was exactly what he'd been thinking about Lily.

He wasn't one hundred percent sold on the suggested random violence or mistaken identity theories the investigator had mentioned. Nor was he sold on the idea that tonight's attack had been an act of revenge by a former collar.

So, had tonight's attack been meant for Cam? Or Lily?

It would have been easy enough to follow either one of them here.

The key puzzle piece that continued to spin through Cam's mind was whether or not Lily had heard something when her call connected with Nicole's phone. Was the shock of her sister's murder keeping her from remembering?

Out there somewhere, the murderer had Nicole's phone, and he had Lily's name.

In Cam's gut he knew the killer more than likely believed Lily to be a threat. As long as that killer was on the loose, Cam intended to stick like glue to the woman, no matter what his partner or lieutenant might think.

Suddenly, keeping Lily safe took priority over solving the case. While Cam didn't want to waste time analyzing that shift in thinking, he planned to follow his gut. And right now, his gut was telling him to focus on Lily.

He'd put her on the receiving end of round-the-clock surveillance, whether she liked it or not.

He moved toward Lily and the dog, reaching out to ruffle the top of Trouble's head.

"You sure he's okay?"

Lily nodded. "Not a scratch. He must have squeezed through the fence and stayed gone until the chaos died down."

Cam said nothing, although he had to admit the intense relief he'd felt at the sight of the dog had taken him by surprise.

He must be going soft.

Cam shifted his stare to the ruins of the brownstone and bit back a groan. The most important thing was that he and Lily had scrambled to safety and Trouble had survived. The same couldn't be said for his daughter's drawings—the prized possessions he treasured more than anything else in the apartment.

Hell, truth was there wasn't much else in the apartment *but* his daughter's drawings. But, to Cam, they were priceless. And now they were gone.

His throat tightened as he realized how much he was going to miss walking through that front door every night.

"Are you okay?" Lily's concerned tone pulled him out of his thoughts and back into the moment.

He shoved away the images of his daughter's artwork—a house, a dog, a pony—and focused instead on Lily's face and the spot on her cheek where a dark smudge marred her flawless skin.

He reached for her, rubbing away the soot with his thumb. Some small sense of satisfaction rose in his chest as her throat worked in response to his touch.

"I was going to ask you whether you wanted to go to your place or mine—" he tipped his chin toward the hollowed-out shell "—but I'm thinking I need to rephrase the question."

To his surprise, Lily reached her hand up to cover his, intertwining her fingers with his. "I can't believe I'm about to say this, but I'm relieved your arrogance survived intact. Let's go."

LILY AND CAM SAT IN the safe-house kitchen, saying little and eating heartily. Lily hadn't thought herself hungry after all that had happened in the past few days, but once Kyle whipped up one of his famous triple-decker sandwiches, she realized otherwise. She'd downed almost an entire half before her brain kicked into gear, reliving what had happened.

She flashed back to the moments on Cam's patio. The moments in which she'd seen Cam as a man, and not as a hard-nosed detective. Understanding dawned inside her as she pictured the crayon drawings hung prominently in his home, the way he moved in the kitchen as if he'd fended for himself forever.

Cameron Hughes was a man very much alone. He could put on a good show in front of other officers, in front of Lily, in front of the media, but Lily had the sense that behind the door to his brownstone, Cam was simply a father who had lost his daughter, a man who had lost his way.

He had the hard shell to prove it. She should know. She wore a similar tough coating.

Lily had never trusted her heart. Had never trusted anyone. Not anyone except her family, that is, and now The Body Hunters. Life was safer with your head buried in a ledger sheet. Nicole had always given Lily a hard time about her refusal to put her heart on the line, but she'd tried hard to understand, as only a sister could.

Nicole.

Lily's heart twisted and she set the second half of her sandwich back on her plate, untouched.

Kyle had left the kitchen as soon as he'd served the sandwiches, intuitively sensing the shift between Lily and Cam. They needed time alone before the team met to debrief on the day, whether they spoke to each other or not. Cam and Lily simply needed to be. After all, they were two people who had shared a life-changing experience—an apparent attempt on their lives.

"No appetite?" Cam's tone was softer than Lily thought possible. "You should eat more."

"I ate half." She forced a smile. "And you're starting to sound like Silvia."

The older woman had hovered around the two of them like a mother hen before she'd taken Trouble and vanished, claiming he needed a bath. Trouble hadn't minded one bit. As a matter of fact, if dogs could smile, he'd been beaming from the attention he'd received upon their return to the safe house.

Cam shook his head. "I was thinking I sounded more like Kyle. He watches every move you make."

That got her attention. Lily studied him, searching the depths of his gray gaze for the true meaning of what he'd said. Was he jealous of Kyle? A bubble of warmth burst inside her at the thought.

This time when she smiled, the move was genuine. "Kyle's like the brother I never had. He doesn't watch me. He watches out for me."

"You've known each other a long time?"

Lily gave a quick shrug. "A few years. Next to Martin, I'm the newest member on the team. The others—" she tipped her head toward the hall "—they've been together forever. Especially Rick and Will, whom you haven't met. They founded The Body Hunters twenty years ago."

Her words left Cam visibly surprised, and he fell silent.

She knew what he was thinking. If one group existed, how many more must? And chances were those that existed weren't all out to save the world, like The Body Hunters.

"I can tell you don't approve." The blunt tone of her voice snapped Cam's attention into focus.

"I'm a police officer, Lily." He leaned toward her, dropping his voice. "Do you expect me to stand up and cheer for a group of vigilantes?"

"We're not like that."

"Then what are you like?"

"Well—" she leaned closer, narrowing the space between them across the tabletop "—until this week, I was the only team member who hadn't suffered a loss, who hadn't become part of the group out of the need to do something positive to compensate for something horribly negative."

"Why did you join?"

"I'm good at what I do and they sought me out for a case." She thinned her lips and sighed. "I never looked back."

"A financial case?" Cam asked.

"Money laundering. International drug running." She tipped her head to one side. "Now it's my turn."

Surprise flashed in his gaze, but he didn't so much as flinch. "Shoot."

"What's her name?"

"Who?" The intense set of his jaw suggested he knew exactly who she meant.

"Your daughter."

"Annie."

"Annie," Lily repeated. "I like it. A little old-fashioned. It suits you."

A smile tugged at the corners of Cam's mouth, and his good looks and love for his daughter hit Lily like a brick between the eyes.

"Are you trying to say I'm old-fashioned?" His smile widened, his tone went uncharacteristically light.

Lily made a show of studying his features, narrowing her eyes and enjoying the moment. "I think I am, Detective Hughes. I think I am."

Silence beat between them for a moment.

"How old is she?" Lily asked.

"Eight." The smile slid from his face.

"And when you and your wife split up?"

"Three."

So he'd been without his little girl for five years. "Do you see her often?"

The light in Cam's eyes faded as if he'd drawn the curtains on his heart. "I don't see her at all. Her mother and her new husband moved to California." Cam pushed out of the chair, carrying both of their plates to the sink. "We'd better get going. No doubt your team's waiting."

Lily blinked. What had just happened? What had she said that pushed Cam away.

She caught herself then, realizing that pushing Cam away was exactly what she needed.

Cam was the man responsible for finding Nicole's killer. He was also a man who believed Nicole had brought about her own death with her thirst for fame.

Just contemplating that reality cooled any momentary attraction Lily might have felt.

She stood, moving quickly toward the kitchen door. "You're right, of course. I'm sorry I asked."

I'M SORRY I ASKED. The strained tone of Lily's words hung in Cam's mind as he stood in the empty kitchen, leaning hard against the sink.

What had just happened? For a brief moment, he'd let Lily see a part of him he'd never so much as shown his own partner.

Annie.

Just saying the name had been like a knife through his heart.

Old-fashioned.

He thought about what Lily had said and realized she was right. Cam was old-fashioned. So old-fashioned he'd believed a man's job was to work as hard as he could to provide for his family.

The thing was, he'd never learned that providing meant more than handing over money. Providing meant drawing a line between your cases and your loved ones. Providing meant making time to be a father.

Providing meant making time to play with your child, to read bedtime stories, to sit and talk with your wife.

Providing meant being all the things Cam knew he wasn't capable of being.

He wasn't wired that way. The reality stung, but it was the reality just the same.

He hadn't wanted to spend time with a woman—really spend time with a woman—until he met Lily. What was it about her that drew him in?

He must be losing his edge. The answer was that simple.

Cam took a deep breath before he headed into the hall toward the case room. He wouldn't make the mistake of letting Lily direct another conversation toward his personal life.

His personal life and their professional investigation were two very separate things.

He intended to keep them that way.

"HERE HE IS NOW," RICK SAID as Cam entered the room.

Cam nodded and slid into a chair.

"I was just telling them you never had the chance to fill me in on the autopsy report." Lily shifted in her seat and rubbed her face.

Her grief and exhaustion had begun to take a heavy toll.

Cam nodded, leaning back against his seat. "The method's off." He delivered the line flatly, enjoying the range of reactions on the other faces.

"So Grey didn't kill my sister?" Lily pushed to her feet.

Cam held his ground. "I never said that. I said the method's off. The cuts are identical, the pattern the same, but your sister was dead before he cut her. She died of strangulation."

His words registered and the horrible possibility of hearing her sister's fight for life played out in the depths of Lily's eyes.

"Why would he do that?" Her question sounded barely above a whisper.

"Maybe he didn't have the control he wanted." Kyle's voice cut into the mix, followed by Rick's.

"Or maybe the killer wasn't Grey at all. Maybe it was a copycat."

Lily lowered her face to her hands for a split second, then straightened. "So what do we do next to sort this all out?"

"Well—" Cam leaned back and crossed his legs ankle-to-knee "—you could let the police do their jobs."

Rick carried on as if Cam hadn't spoken a word. "Martin, progress on the photo enhancement?"

Martin stood, moving to project a huge copy of the image onto the wall. Call Cam crazy, but he didn't see a shred of improvement…at first. Then Martin systematically explained the enhancements and progressions of the restoration. The image was still unrecognizable, but Cam had to admit, the kid knew what he was doing.

"How much longer?" he asked.

"Tough to say." Martin shrugged. "Could be four to five more days. Could take weeks."

Well, that narrowed things down.

"Silvia's got something interesting in the Sizemore death," Rick continued.

The older woman stood and clicked at a laptop computer until a series of screens appeared on the one blank wall. "Someone's been making monthly calls to Gladys Sizemore for the past four years."

"Set day and time?" Lily asked.

"Saturday nights." Silvia pointed to the highlighted entries in the log of incoming calls. "Every Saturday night except last."

"The night she died." Cam spoke the words as if thinking out loud. He sat forward. "But they're not all from the same number."

"Very good, Detective." Silvia's expression brightened. The woman obviously loved the kick she got from uncovering data. "They are all from prepaid cell phone numbers, however."

"Traceable only to the location of purchase," Martin said, his tone climbing.

"A new number every month," Silvia continued. "Each purchased at a different prepaid provider."

Cam sat back, playing devil's advocate. "Who's to say she didn't have a friend or family member who preferred prepaid calls?"

"According to my info," Silvia continued, "Gladys Sizemore had no family left alive, unless Tracey survived out there somewhere."

Lily scrambled to her feet. "My sister called her five times in the two weeks before her death. Sizemore obviously had a story Nicole wanted."

"And what else do you see?" Silvia asked.

"An extra call using the same prepaid number as the month before." Excitement popped in Martin's voice.

"Exactly."

"The day after my sister's fourth call." Lily wrapped her arms around her waist.

"What if Sizemore was sharing information our prepaid caller didn't want her to share?" Silvia asked.

"And he or she showed up in person instead of calling?" Cam reached for his pocket and groaned when he came up with the pack of gum.

The team might work nicely together, but rule number one was not letting your imagination take over. They failed miserably.

"We need to find out who made those calls." Lily shot Cam a glare, apparently reading the sarcasm in his last statement.

"Suggestions?" Rick asked.

"We could start with the camp." Cam stepped away from his chair and approached the whiteboard.

If he wanted to make sure the team didn't muck up his case, he might as well start guiding their actions now. He pointed to one word. *Providence.* "I called the precinct in charge of the original investigation. Providence Mills."

"And?" Lily narrowed her eyes.

"And the evidence went missing years ago. The chief there claims they've moved offices a number of times."

"But you want to pay a face-to-face visit." Kyle's typically serious expression broke into a grin.

Cam was struck at that moment by how the team members played off of each other, their thoughts and ideas respected, considered. They worked like a well-oiled investigative unit—an overly imaginative unit—but a cohesive unit just the same.

"We can be there first thing the day after tomorrow." Hope sounded in Lily's voice.

Cam didn't have to ask why tomorrow would be out. They all knew the answer to that question. Tomorrow, Lily and her family would bury their daughter, their sister, their friend.

"I think that's enough for tonight." Rick stood, effectively dismissing the meeting. "Long day tomorrow. Early start."

Kyle, Silvia and Martin all filed out of the room.

Rick crossed to where Cam stood and shook his hand. "Good to have you here, Detective. I can understand that you might not appreciate our logic, but I assure you we know what we're doing."

"It's late." Lily stood and stretched after Rick and the other team members had filtered out of the room. "You rescued me from a fire tonight. I'd say that deserves a place to stay. There's a pull-out cot in my room. You're welcome to it."

Cam's mouth answered before his brain kicked in. "I'd appreciate that." He could call Vince and tell him he'd move into his spare bedroom tomorrow. For now, Lily had a point.

Cam was exhausted.

He wanted nothing more than to catch a few hours of sleep before he hit the case hard again tomorrow. Plus, staying at the safe house provided the extra bonus of making keeping an eye on Lily an easy assignment.

She hesitated at the door without turning to face him. "I'm sorry about Annie's drawings. I know they can't be replaced."

Lily was gone before Cam could form a response.

He gave her a head start for the bedroom, staying in the case room analyzing the facts as they were.

He put a call in to Vince. There was still no word on Grey. No movement. No sightings. No private citizens coming forward with tips.

He'd never seen a case go so cold, so fast.

A short while later, Cam pushed open the door to the bedroom Lily had offered to share. Her sleeping form lay fully clothed on the bed.

Cam stepped close enough to watch her, to study the now-calm features that had been nothing but stressed and tense since the moment she'd first walked into the precinct.

Exhaustion. Sleep.

The body's own mode of self-preservation.

A person could only operate on caffeine and adrenaline for so long before she shut down.

Cam reached for the blanket Lily had draped across the cot, no doubt for him. He unfolded the fleece and spread it over her, letting his fingertips trail across her shoulder, reaching to brush the hair from her face.

Then he did something he hadn't done in over five years. He crawled into bed next to a woman. More aptly, he crawled on top of the bed, on top of the blanket, but he reached for her, enfolding Lily into his arms. She moved closer, tucking against his body as if she knew he wanted nothing more than to keep her safe.

Yet, as the warmth of Lily's body permeated the cold recesses of Cam's heart, he knew he no longer had to worry about crossing the line between professional and personal.

He had only to worry about how to cross back.

Chapter Eight

Body Clock: 67:30

The Man watched as the mourners swarmed around the casket, lowering their long-stemmed roses to the casket as if the dead reporter had earned them. Nicole Christides had lived for moments identical to this one.

Sensational moments.

Heart-wrenching moments.

Human drama scripted for the camera.

Oh, how she would have loved this story. Her story.

Maybe somewhere she was smiling down—or up—at her own funeral. Now that, he could picture.

He glanced toward Detective Hughes.

According to the local media, Hughes had lost everything in last night's firebombing, yet they'd kept the details to a minimum. That disappointed The Man, almost as much as the good detective's survival.

He shifted his focus to Nicole's younger sister, Lily. According to the news reports, she'd been with the detective at the time of the explosion.

A pity.

If things had worked out, two concerns might have been eliminated for the price of one, so to speak.

He studied the lines of her face, the curve of her cheek, her slender neck.

Breathtaking, actually.

He hadn't seen her since the night outside her parents' store. Had she thought about him? Wondered who he was? Worried about what might have happened if the good detective hadn't appeared at the crucial moment?

A longing stirred deep inside him, but he willed it away. He was not a killer. At least, not by choice. He was a killer by necessity, and necessity alone.

And until he heard otherwise, he had no reason to eliminate Lily Christides, as much as he'd love to wrap his fingers around her neck.

He'd poured over every news article detailing the investigation into Nicole's murder, and not one had mentioned the sister's incoming phone call. He'd also used his carefully acquired connections to check with someone in the know at the investigating precinct. They'd heard nothing.

It appeared fate had smiled on him once again.

The younger Christides would go back to Seattle and he'd have nothing to worry about. End of story.

A pang of regret slid through him. As pleased as he was that she hadn't heard him kill her sister, another part of him found the prospect of eliminating her quite thrilling.

He tamped down that particular urge and shifted his focus to the detective. Hughes scanned the crowd like a hawk waiting for an unsuspecting rabbit to scamper past. Did he honestly expect the killer to walk up and introduce himself?

But then, as The Man followed the line of the detective's

gaze, he realized Hughes looked not at the crowd, but rather at the same mourner The Man had been studying.

Lily Christides.

The Man should have known. He couldn't decide if he were pleased by the fact there might be an attraction brewing, or if he were concerned. No. He did a mental headshake. Not concerned.

Annoyed.

The good people of Philadelphia were paying the detective to work, not to chase the victim's sister. Although, a distracted detective might certainly work to The Man's advantage.

Hughes looked in The Man's direction and held his gaze momentarily before looking away.

The detective's expression showed no recognition of who The Man was or what he'd done. Perhaps Hughes wasn't as sharp as he'd like everyone to think.

For now, The Man was in the clear.

And he had every intention of staying that way.

"ANYTHING?" CAM SPOKE SUBTLY into his earpiece, then waited for Vince's response.

"Nope. Lovely day for a funeral, though. At least I get to work on my tan."

Cam winced at his partner's words and refocused on the crowd.

He wasn't surprised there was no sign of Grey. The man wasn't stupid enough to show up at the funeral, but it was standard procedure to be ready, just in case. The department had a small presence, although Cam had to admit they stuck out like sore thumbs.

Try as they might, the team hadn't had one break in

tracking Buddy Grey's movements since he'd left a halfway house. His mother swore she'd had no contact from her son, but Cam found that difficult to believe. Even if she had heard from Buddy, what mother was likely to rat out her own son? Especially a son she'd always believed innocent.

Cam's mind wandered to the destruction of his home as he continued to scan the crowd. His gaze settled on Lily and he thought again of how it had felt to wake up with the brunette beauty in his arms.

If anything had happened to her…well…the intensity of emotion evoked by the thought stole his breath away.

The arson investigator had confirmed earlier that morning that the signature of the materials used to destroy Cam's home matched those used by a local gang.

The bombing apparently had nothing to do with Nicole's death and everything to do with Cam and Vince's recent case against two of the gang's leaders.

He shook his focus back to the funeral and the crowd of mourners.

Nicole's final farewell had attracted more than loved ones. The service had attracted a who's who of local politicians, celebrities and media personalities. He supposed the reporter really had been on her way up.

Too bad she never made it.

He bit back a snarl as he caught the eye of Tim Fitzsimmons, executive director of Rebuild Philadelphia.

The man stood front and center, the picture of the perfect grieving boyfriend, even though it was common knowledge he and Nicole had only recently started dating.

Fitzsimmons was no doubt more than aware of the media cameras lurking nearby, albeit at a tasteful distance.

As the graveside service concluded, Fitzsimmons made

a move in Cam's direction. Cam groaned, but knew this was the perfect opportunity to ask a few questions.

He'd never liked the man even though his work to build affordable housing for those in need had been frequently cited as a model for the rest of the nation.

All good on the surface.

Fitzsimmons approached and Cam shook his hand, biting back his personal dislike.

His mother had once told him she need only look in someone's eyes to know whether or not they could be trusted.

Cam looked into Tim Fitzsimmons's eyes now and didn't like what he saw.

"My sympathies." Cam clasped a hand on Tim's shoulder. "She didn't deserve this."

Tim nodded. "I want five minutes alone with the bastard once they get him in custody."

Cam might have believed Fitzsimmons truly cared if the emotions of his words had been reflected in his eyes.

"How long had you two been dating?"

"Are you asking as a friend, or cop?"

Fitzsimmons would never be what Cam called a friend, but he wasn't about to say anything of the sort. "Does it matter?"

Fitzsimmons narrowed his gaze suspiciously. "Nicole and I had been dating for weeks."

"Two weeks? Three weeks? Six weeks?"

Fitzsimmons tensed. "Are you suggesting our dating had something to do with her death?"

Now there was a mental leap fit for a guilty conscience. "I'm an investigator, Fitzsimmons. Asking questions is who I am."

The other man studied him momentarily before he responded. "Sometimes love transcends days and weeks, Detective. Perhaps you'll get the privilege of finding that out someday."

"Perhaps." Cam nodded toward where Mayor Langston Montgomery and the city's director of external affairs, Ross Patterson, stood. "Looks like you weren't the only one who decided to put in an appearance for the press."

"I loved her, Hughes. I could care less about the press."

But as Fitzsimmons walked away, Cam knew better. The murdered reporter's funeral would be one of the media events of the year.

Fitzsimmons was savvy enough to know his popularity ratings would soar if he played the grief factor well. And popularity was something he'd need in the months ahead. He served at the pleasure of the mayor—the mayor who had opted not to run for reelection, leaving the path wide open for his right-hand man, Patterson, to inherit city hall.

The reality was that Tim's six-figure job might be a thing of the past the moment the new mayor breezed into office, even though the two had been friends most of their adult lives.

Cam studied Fitzsimmons's body language as he walked past Mayor Montgomery and Patterson. He nodded to the first and snubbed the second. Patterson carefully timed a comment to one of the mayor's bodyguards, allowing him to avoid Fitzsimmons altogether.

Something had happened to drive the friends apart. Cam just hadn't figured out what. Not yet.

He waited until Fitzsimmons moved out of sight before he scanned the crowd again. His gaze settled on Lily.

Oh, who was he kidding? His gaze had been settling on Lily all day.

After seeing her in jeans and a T-shirt the day before, seeing her today had served as a stark reminder both of the fact she'd lost her sister, and of the fact she was one hell of a beautiful woman. He'd be wise to focus on the first observation and steer clear of the second.

Never one to do the safe thing, he pressed his earpiece and spoke. "Going to express my condolences."

He ignored the wise aleck remark Vince shot back in return.

Cam had taken a few steps toward the Christides family when Patterson and his entourage stepped into Cam's line of view. He held back, waiting until the up-and-coming politician finished paying his respects and stepped away.

Yet when Patterson stopped to glance back in Lily's direction, an odd emotion bubbled deep inside Cam's gut. Jealousy? Protectiveness?

He didn't like the way the man eyed her, and yet, could he blame him? She was stunning, even in her grief.

He felt Lily's gaze before their eyes met and held. Sadness edged the corners of her eyes and Cam's heart caught. Not exactly the reaction of an objective detective, but then, objectivity had gone out the window the day he'd first met the woman.

A smart man would nod and turn away.

Instead, Cam closed the space between them, his stare never leaving Lily's.

LILY AND HER FATHER STOOD on either side of her mother, ready to lend their support if needed. The matriarch of the Christides family was known for remaining stoic and unflappable under pressure.

Today proved to be no different. No wonder Lily cringed at the thought of showing any form of weakness.

A steady stream of mourners paid their respects, filing past Nicole's casket after the closing prayer had been offered.

The July sun sat high in the afternoon sky, unforgiving in its strength and intensity. Dark suits and somber expressions were the uniform of the day and, even if some of the emotions offered were for nothing more than show, Nicole would have loved the outpouring on her behalf.

Lily shifted in her uncomfortable high heels, longing to slip into her jeans and a T-shirt. Better still, she'd take a nightshirt and a very dark room.

The past several days had taken their toll and she felt as though she was running on fumes.

She thought momentarily of waking inside Cam's arms this morning. Her own surprise had been matched by the look on the detective's face. He'd hemmed and hawed, saying she'd looked cold during the night.

Lily hadn't believed him, but she had to admit she'd enjoyed the moment before they'd both realized where they were and who they were with.

She'd felt safe in his arms, as much as the independent woman in her hated to admit the fact. She fought the urge to close her eyes and savor the remembered feel of his body next to hers, one arm draped across her hip, the length of his leg pressed against her own.

"It's a pleasure to meet you." A deep voice roused Lily from the images emblazoned on her memory. She focused on the man before her, frowning a bit at her lack of recognition.

"Ross Patterson." He extended a hand to give Lily's a quick shake. "Your sister was to be an integral part of the upcoming election. We had several profiles planned. My deepest condolences."

Lily nodded. "Thank you. It's an honor to meet you."

"I only wish it were under better circumstances." He turned to study the casket, his gaze holding just a moment too long, Lily thought. Dramatic effect? Or had he been one of the many high-powered men with whom her sister had become involved at one point or another?

"You knew her well?" Lily asked.

Patterson shook his head. "Not as well as I would have liked to. She had a bright future ahead of her."

Lily nodded, expecting Patterson to move on down the line, but he didn't.

"How long will you be staying in our fair city?" he asked.

Lily hesitated before she answered, oddly unnerved by the tone of the man's voice. Her imagination and fatigue had begun to wreak havoc. "I have a few things to help my family with here, then I'll be going back to Seattle."

As she watched the man walk away, she couldn't help but wonder why a powerful politician like Ross Patterson would care about her plans?

He stopped a few feet away, turned to face her again and smiled.

"Handsome man." Her mother's soft voice tickled Lily's ear, yet it was something different that captured her attention.

Cam strode across the lawn, headed straight for them. He paid his respects, then led Lily a few feet away.

Lily fought the urge to wrap her arms around his neck and bury her face against his chest.

Her pulse quickened.

Fatigue. Surely she could chalk every one of these uncharacteristic thoughts up to fatigue.

Cam's eyes narrowed. "How are you holding up?"

"Fine." Lily lied. "Just fine."

His eyebrows lifted knowingly. "You must be the most stubborn woman I've ever met."

A smile pulled at Lily's lips. "Coming from you, I'll take that as a compliment." They stood in companionable silence for a few seconds. "Any news today?"

Cam made a snapping noise with his mouth. "Seems my recent firebombing was courtesy of our local gangs at work."

Lily nodded. "Considerate of them."

"You?" he asked.

She shook her head. "Nothing. No movement on Grey. No more progress on the photo, apparently."

Cam frowned. They were getting nowhere.

The mourners had thinned, leaving no one at her sister's graveside.

Lily stared at Nicole's casket, wondering how she could bring herself to lower the rose she clutched in her fist. How could she bring herself to say goodbye and walk away?

Cam closed one hand around her elbow. "I'll walk with you."

Relief and gratitude whispered through her.

She set the single rose on the teetering pile, kissed her fingertips and pressed them to the gleaming casket.

Her parents waited inside the limousine as the car sat idling. "I'll see you tomorrow?" She posed the statement as a question.

Cam nodded, letting his hand fall to his side. Lily's elbow felt oddly cool where his fingers had been.

She turned to walk away, but stopped, looking back over her shoulder. "Thank you."

Something shimmered in the depths of his eyes, something far, far removed from the uninvolved stare of a police detective.

She didn't steal another glance at Detective Hughes until she sat inside the limo as the vehicle pulled away from the side of the road.

Cam remained unmoved, watching her still, and her stomach tightened.

The detective continued to surprise her with glimpses of the heart beneath his arrogance.

As he faded from her sight, she realized that, for all of her training and experience in matters of finance, hostage search, and criminal investigation, matters of the heart were something for which she was totally unprepared.

CAM WATCHED AS THE FAMILY limousine pulled away. He couldn't deny the sense of protectiveness growing inside him, try as he might.

Lily had tapped into a part of him he'd thought long dead—the part that cared about someone outside of his case load.

Yet as much as he wanted to comfort Lily in her grief, he wasn't the one she needed. She needed her family, and family he wasn't.

Not to Lily.

Not to anyone.

The reality served as a sound reminder of why he had spent the past five years avoiding all emotional entanglements. He was no good at anything but the job. Plain and simple.

"See you tomorrow." He spoke the words to no one as the limousine slipped out of sight. Then he waited until the cemetery workers moved in, taking over at the gravesite now that every last mourner had vanished.

Out there somewhere, Buddy Grey walked free whil
Nicole's casket waited to be lowered into the ground.

Cam couldn't turn back the clock, couldn't spare Lil
and her family their heartache, but he could make Grey pa
for what he'd done.

This time, there would be no room for error.

Chapter Nine

Cam stepped into the briefing room fifteen minutes late. He'd sat outside the Christides house nursing a cup of stale coffee, telling himself he was doing his job. But what had he been waiting for? An appearance by the killer? A glimpse of Lily?

The minute he set foot back inside the precinct, his inner turmoil kicked to life. For someone who played by the book, he'd done nothing but break procedure since Lily had entered his life.

"Hughes." Lieutenant Casey stepped away from his position at the front of the room, heading straight for Cam. "My office. Now."

Sonofa— Cam scowled, but did as he'd been told. He had a pretty good idea of what was coming.

Vince made a move to intercept him, but one sharp look from the lieutenant stopped him in his tracks. "Alone."

Once they entered his office, Casey didn't so much as take a seat before he launched into his tirade. "You're off of this case. Effective immediately."

Cam fought the urge to talk back, knowing from experience he'd only make things worse.

"Did you honestly think you could break jurisdiction, interject yourself into another case and I wouldn't find out about it?" He barreled on without taking a breath. "And how about this case? You missed the last briefing. You're late today? What the hell's going on, Hughes? If I didn't know better, I'd think you want a suspension."

Cam knew the lieutenant was technically correct, but Cam planned to blow the case wide open. He couldn't get kicked off now. "I'm going to break this thing. I can feel it."

Casey shook his head. "I don't need you to feel anything. You have an investigation to keep under control, a murderer to put back behind bars and a job to keep. Am I making myself clear?"

"Crystal."

"Have you crossed the line?"

Cam narrowed his eyes.

"I saw you with the victim's sister at the funeral." He jerked a thumb back toward the room they'd left. "We all saw you. And I know for a fact you're not following protocol, and you're not filing reports on whatever it is you're up to. You've got twenty-four hours to clean up your act, Hughes, or you'll not only be off the case, you'll be back on a desk. Understood?"

The lieutenant closed the space between them, leaning so close Cam could smell the onions from his afternoon cheese steak on his breath. "Take a walk, Hughes. Then get back to work."

Anger blurred Cam's vision, but he held his tongue for once in his life. Cam jerked the lieutenant's office door open so sharply, it slammed against the wall as he stormed out.

He seethed with anger, yet as he pushed out of the precinct door into the warm evening, a calm sense of purpose overtook him. He walked, passing his parked car, passing the burned out shell of his home.

He walked without direction and yet with a very definite destination.

He headed for the place where everything had started. The murder. The investigation. His involvement with Lily. His loss of focus. His sudden disregard for procedure, for process.

As he rounded the street corner, light spilled from inside Nicole Christides's brownstone, bringing one question to the forefront of Cam's mind.

With Lily's family immersed in funeral activities, who on earth was inside? And why?

THE MAN HAD BROKEN AWAY from the crowd long enough to lose them, long enough to lose himself, following the younger Christides away from the cemetery. He'd thought about paying his respects at her parents' home, but he was too smart for that. Far, far too smart.

And so he waited. And now he'd been rewarded.

Lily drove alone to her sister's brownstone. She climbed the steps, stepped around the crime-scene tape, and unlocked the front door.

Images from the night of the murder filled his vision, filled his senses. Standing at the door, cradling the flower basket in his arm. Watching Nicole's eyes fill with wonder—and then with fear—as she recognized him, recognized his purpose.

He wondered how her sister would react under the same circumstances.

The younger sister seemed more self-aware, more willing to fight back. He'd had just a small taste of her physical prowess when she'd dodged him outside her parents' shop.

What was she doing now? Searching for memories? For evidence? What?

He pictured the sweep of the hallway beneath the archway from the foyer to the kitchen, and wondered where Lily was inside the house.

He longed to step inside, longed to relive the moment of Nicole's death, longed to re-create the scene. He moved closer and closer still, scanning the street for signs of other pedestrians but finding none.

He should walk past the building, but he didn't. He couldn't.

He hesitated instead, his forward motion halted. He studied the house and the glow of light from inside, and thought of the sister waiting, unaware that he watched her, wanted her, needed her.

Only out of necessity, he reminded himself.

He killed for purpose, and purpose only.

He should go. He should leave this place.

This kill wasn't necessary. Not yet.

But then, instead of walking away, The Man decided to stay.

CAM SLOWED HIS PACE AS HE drew near to the steps leading to the home's front door. The crime-scene tape had fallen to the brick, ripped apart by the family or a cleaning crew, no doubt. His focus lifted to the windows and the glow of light from inside.

He studied the pattern of light. Dark upstairs, bright hallway and rooms to one side of the downstairs. The kitchen and office, perhaps, if he were remembering correctly.

Of course, whoever was inside could be a family

member, but he thought it unlikely. Not on the evening after the funeral.

A shadow moved beyond the windows framing from the front door, and Cam reached for his weapon, unsnapping the safety straps on his holster.

It was no cliché that killers often returned to the scene of the crime. They couldn't help themselves.

Maybe Nicole's killer had decided tonight would be the perfect time to relive what he'd done.

Cam should be so lucky.

Adrenaline rushed through his veins as he took the front steps one at a time, silently. Moving in.

Chances were he might be about to find someone fully expected to be inside the home, but if Cam had to choose between overreacting and getting caught without his weapon at the ready, he'd choose the former.

LILY STOOD IN THE CENTER of what had been her sister's kitchen and willed herself to feel something. Anything.

But after today, after the funeral, the condolences and the long line of mourners paying their respects both at the graveside and at her parents' house, Lily found she couldn't feel anything at all.

She dropped to her knees and traced a hand across the kitchen floor. If she didn't have first-hand knowledge of the fact a horrific crime had taken place here, she'd never guess the fact.

Professional cleaners had come through as soon as the scene had been released to the family. Her parents had been here yesterday to begin the process of packing up Nicole's life, but they'd been unable to get any work done.

The violence and the loss were too fresh, too raw.

Matter of fact, the loss of her sister was the one thing Lily *could* feel inside the house. Without Nicole the house felt more than empty, it felt forsaken. Every last inch.

Lily straightened, running her hand along the quartz kitchen counter Nicole had insisted upon installing. Only the latest and greatest would do during the home's recent renovations.

Lily contrasted the image with thoughts of Cam's kitchen and living room—the butcher block counter, the brick wall, the crayon drawings.

As tough as the man tried to appear, the small glimpse she'd witnessed of his life suggested otherwise. Not to mention the fact she'd woken up safely wrapped in his embrace.

Lily shook her head as she stepped away from the counter. What on earth was she doing? Standing in the middle of her sister's kitchen judging not only the countertop, but also the depth of Detective Hughes's heart?

She needed to get a grip. And now.

Lily stepped back into the hall and headed for Nicole's office, snapping on a light as she entered the pristine space. Her sister's laptop had been taken into evidence, but the flat screen monitor for her desktop system sat in the middle of an otherwise spotless desk.

No family photos lined the walls or shelves of the built-in bookcase. Nothing here hinted at the once bright personality her sister had possessed. Here, Lily witnessed only the driving ambition that had defined her sister's life.

Lily tipped her head to scan the book titles on the shelves. *Understanding the Criminal Mind. Living Your Dream. Achieving the Life You've Always Wanted.*

She smiled when her gaze lit on a shelf devoted entirely to celebrity biographies.

No one could ever say her sister hadn't dreamed big. Too bad she never got to see her dreams come true. Nicole's had been a young life erased before she could make her mark.

Check that. She had made one mark—the release of Buddy Grey. Had the man killed her? Was Cam correct in his conviction?

Frustration and grief tangled inside Lily and her vision blurred. She wiped away the moisture, closed her eyes momentarily, and breathed deeply to regain her composure.

When she looked again, she spotted an object very much out of place in the picture-perfect office.

A ballerina music box.

Grief and loss wrapped their fingers around Lily's heart and squeezed.

Their parents had given each of the sisters a music box the night before they'd started first grade. Lily couldn't believe Nicole still had hers, let alone displayed it prominently in the otherwise sterile office. Maybe her sister hadn't lost touch with her down-to-earth roots after all.

The thought made Lily's heart twist more sharply in her chest.

She lifted the delicate object down from the shelf, pulled open the tiny door and watched as the ballerina spun, letting the tinny, off-key tune carry her back to a happier time.

Then Lily slid open the secret drawer, as she'd always called it. She could remember hiding priceless possessions in hers. A lucky penny. A favorite ring. The first love note she'd ever received.

But the memories evaporated when she saw what sat inside. A small chrome object. A flash drive.

The present edged out the past, and Lily plucked the portable storage device from the drawer, cupping it in her palm.

Why had Nicole stashed the device in such an odd spot?

There was only one way to find out.

She'd taken one step back toward the desk when something sounded from the hall.

A floorboard creaked. Then another.

What the—? Hadn't she locked the front door?

Someone had entered behind her, but who? An innocent person seeking shelter? A reporter? The killer?

Lily glanced around the room, searching for a weapon and settling on a heavy stapler. She tucked the flash drive into the pocket of her skirt, held the stapler at the ready and stepped behind the door to wait.

The footfalls drew nearer and her pulse began a rapid tapping in her ears.

Whoever crossed that threshold was in for a surprise, and a battle, if need be. Lily might not be armed in the traditional sense, but she was trained in self-defense. There was no time like the present to test her skills.

She pulled her body back against the wall, like a coil ready to spring. Then she spotted the phone on Nicole's desk.

A call to 9-1-1 was even more intelligent than planning her defense.

But the warbling of a different phone startled her and she lost her balance, crashing hard against the corner of the wall. She bit back a cry.

"Sonofa—"

The phone fell silent, the ringer apparently depressed by whoever had sworn aloud.

Lily squinted, playing the voice back in her head. A

mixture of recognition and disbelief played through her, but she held her position just in case.

"Cam?"

"Lily?"

She stepped from behind the door, revealing herself. "What in the hell are you doing here?" Heat fired in her cheeks, and she winced at the show of embarrassment. "You scared me half to death." She still held the stapler in a white-knuckled grip, waving it as she spoke.

"That was your plan?" He walked toward her, not even trying to hide a grin. "You were going to hit me with that?" He reached for the stapler, wrapping his fingers around her hand as he pulled her arm toward him.

Lily watched his moves, her eyes locked on their joined hands until her gaze snapped up to his. Something danced in the depths of his gaze, jolting her to the core. If she wasn't mistaken, the disdain she'd spotted there when they'd first met had been soundly pushed aside by a far different emotion. Desire.

"Why are you here?" His voice dropped low, his grasp held.

She pulled her hand free of his grip, then set the stapler back on the desk. "I already asked you the same thing."

Cam shrugged before he walked over to Nicole's desk, tracing his fingertips across the polished expanse of wood, visibly devoid of loose papers, file folders, notepads.

"I don't know." He blew out a sigh. "I started walking and I ended up here. I spotted the lights and thought Grey had come back."

She focused on the first part of what he'd said. Concern flooded through her, surprising her with its intensity. "Are you all right?"

He stepped so close she could feel the heat of his body. Lily's throat worked and her stomach tightened. She longed to reach out to him, to touch his cheek, but instead she did nothing. Nothing but stare.

Cam's tone grew even more gentle. "You mean other than having only a burned out shell to call home and being twenty-four hours away from a suspension?" His forced smile didn't reach his eyes. "I'm fine."

Lily opened her mouth to speak, but Cam kissed her so quickly she didn't have time to do anything but kiss him back.

There was nothing tentative about his move. His kiss was as arrogant as the man, and the pressure of his lips on hers awakened a long-dead need deep inside Lily.

He eased his tongue between her lips and pulled her so tightly against his body that nothing—absolutely nothing—was left to her imagination. For one crazy moment, she thought about letting him take her right there, right then on top of Nicole's pristine desk.

Nicole.

Reality hit Lily like a slap across the face. What was she doing?

She pushed away from Cam, breaking their contact, turning away from him, not wanting to see the desire in his face, on his features, on his moist lips. Not wanting him to see the same emotion mirrored on her face.

"What are you doing?" she asked.

He shook his head, the move a slow, methodical shake, as if he were wondering the same thing. "I have no idea." He shrugged, his gaze never wavering from hers. "Maybe I just wanted to get that out of the way."

A sharp laugh slid across Lily's lips. "They should print that on a greeting card." She shoved what had just happened out of her head and pulled the flash drive from her pocket, pressing it to Cam's palm.

His brows snapped together. "Where'd you find this?"

"Inside her music box."

He frowned.

"My thoughts exactly." Lily clicked off the office light and stepped into the hall, waiting. "I was going to check it out on her computer, but I'm thinking maybe we should head back to the house. You game?"

He answered her with a grin.

Lily decided then and there to pretend the kiss had never happened. Her thoughts had begun to stray into dangerous territory and she needed to reel them in.

She and Cam were both tired, frustrated and not thinking clearly. The explanation for what had happened was that simple.

She retraced her steps to the kitchen, grabbed her purse and keys and pulled open the front door, locking it after Cam had stepped outside.

He tipped his chin toward the door. "Next time, try locking that when you're on the inside, as well. You never know what sorts might be lurking about."

"Waiting to let themselves in?"

He nodded, still smiling, but the fact he checked the dark sidewalk and street in both directions before they started walking wasn't lost on her.

He held out his hand and Lily frowned. "What?"

"I'll drive."

She handed over the rental car keys without argument, but froze when the small hairs at the nape of her neck lifted.

"Something wrong?" Cam asked.

Lily looked over her shoulder, seeing nothing. "I just had the oddest sense someone's out there."

Cam pulled the passenger door open and ushered her inside. "Someone's most definitely out there. The trick is to find him before he finds us."

THE MAN STOOD IN THE SHADOWS, a thrill racing through him when Lily turned to look in his direction.

Had she sensed him there? Had she been waiting for him? Anticipating his arrival?

Hughes rounded the back of the car and climbed into the driver's seat. So like the detective to refuse to let a woman drive.

Contempt simmered in The Man's gut.

Detective Hughes had been a problem for as long as he could remember. But The Man was smarter. So, so much smarter.

He thought again about the night of the murder, searching his brain, reliving every moment, working to determine whether or not he'd missed anything. Anything at all.

As usual, the only answer he could come up with was nothing.

Nicole Christides's murder had been perfect. Absolutely perfect.

But why should that surprise him? After all, he was very good at what he did.

Very good indeed.

The knowledge soothed him, caressed him.

He waited for the car to pull away from the curb, waiting for the taillights to vanish around the corner. Then he stepped out onto the sidewalk, into plain sight and admired the brownstone, the scene of his perfect crime.

He was in control.

He'd always been in control.

And there was nothing the good detective or Ms. Christides could do to change that.

He'd make very sure of it.

He was in control.

He'd always been in control.

And there was nothing the good detective, Ms. Carlotta, could do to change that.

He'd make very sure of it.

Chapter Ten

Body Clock: 75:35

Lily hadn't said a thing on the way back to the safe house other than to offer directions Cam didn't need. He worked these streets, knew them inside and out, and although he wasn't familiar with the house The Body Hunters now called their temporary home, he certainly knew the locale.

Trouble shot down the hall's center staircase the moment they stepped inside, launching his wiggling body first at Lily and then at Cam.

"He settled in fast," Cam said as he scratched the dog's head.

"Thank goodness." Lily snapped her fingers and the dog jumped to her side, trotting alongside her as she made her way to the kitchen as if he'd been doing so his entire life. "He's such a sweetheart, it breaks my heart every time I think about what he might have heard."

What he might have heard.

Lily's words struck a chord. What had Lily heard? Cam had let the topic fall through the cracks, not like him. He'd let his empathy for the woman conflict with his case. Lieutenant Casey was spot-on. Cam had crossed the line, both physically and emotionally.

Martin barreled out of the case room before Cam could voice his concern about pursuing whatever it was Lily had heard the night of her sister's murder.

"I think I've got something." The younger man's eyes were bright behind his glasses and he grinned so hard, dimples dug into his cheeks.

Ah, the enthusiasm of youth, Cam thought. Give it a few years, buddy. Give it a few years.

"That's fabulous." Lily squeezed Martin's arm then scooped up Trouble. She stopped in her tracks just before she crossed into the other room, her stare locking on Cam. Something flickered in her gaze, a light she quickly extinguished.

She may have gone silent on the topic of their kiss, but apparently the moment hadn't been lost on her.

The kiss had rocked Cam to his toes. He found some small sense of satisfaction in the possibility the shared moment had affected Lily after all.

"Are you staying?" she asked.

Cam nodded, keeping his focus riveted to hers. "Wouldn't miss it." Plus, he had no place else to go, but he wasn't about to say that.

The rest of the team sat gathered downstairs, all eyes focused on a huge projection of the photograph. The subject had become clearer, much clearer. Two kids, no more than teenagers, based on their soft features. A girl and a boy.

"It's Tracey Sizemore." Lily spoke the words in barely more than a whisper. "I find it hard to believe her aunt would have burned a photo of the girl, don't you?"

No one spoke a word, but the team sentiment rang clear. Cam could read each team member's thoughts simply by looking at their eyes. Rick. Kyle. Silvia. Each one's conviction had grown stronger.

They didn't believe Gladys Sizemore had put her treasured photos and papers into the fire. They believed she'd struggled to pull this photo free. Her final act before she died.

Cam suddenly thought of the phone call he'd received in the moments before he'd discovered Lily hiding behind the door of her sister's office.

"Excuse me." He stepped back out of the room, ignoring Lily's curious look.

He pulled up the log of missed calls. His partner, Vince. Not that that should surprise him. Vince had been more than a partner during the past several years. He'd become a friend.

"What's up?" he asked as soon as Vince answered his call.

"I've never seen Casey this pissed." Vince dropped his voice low. "What did you say to him?"

Cam couldn't help but smile. Vince wouldn't believe he'd said nothing, even if he told him. "He gave me twenty-four hours to pull it together," he offered instead.

"The case?"

"My crossing the line with Christides."

Vince blew out a low whistle. "You've been holding out on me?"

Lily peeked out of the case room, brows furrowed. "You all right?" she mouthed.

Cam nodded and she slipped back out of sight.

Had Cam been holding out on Vince? "No," he answered. He'd been holding out on himself, denying himself the chance at loving someone again. Every time he saw Lily smile he knew he'd been a fool to shut himself off all of these years, both from the chance at new love and from the chance at mending his relationship with his daughter. With Annie.

The realization hit him like a ton of bricks and he inhaled sharply.

"You okay, buddy?" Vince's voice snapped Cam's focus back to the call. "Because we may have something," Vince said without waiting to hear Cam's reply.

"On Grey?" Cam's veins hummed with a quickened pulse.

Vince snapped his tongue. "With Sizemore."

"Sizemore?"

"Injection mark."

"Where?" Cam's pulse quickened.

"Base of her neck, at the hairline."

Cam had seen that location used only once before. By a killer trying to cover the needle mark. Had Lily's instincts been right? Had Sizemore been murdered?

"How much longer on the tox screen?" Cam asked.

He suspected one drug in particular that a killer might have used to kill Sizemore quickly. Insulin. Fast-acting and readily available. But without the toxicology results, there was no way to be sure.

"Four days. Your buddy put a rush on it. Says he owes you an apology by the way."

At this point, Cam didn't care. He just wanted those results, and he wanted them a whole lot sooner than four days from now. "They call that a rush?"

"You know how these things work."

Cam could picture the gleam of excitement in Vince's eyes even without seeing him. It was one of the things he admired most about his partner. Vince chased life—and every single case they were handed—as if tomorrow might never come.

Cam scrubbed a hand across his face. Things had just gotten a whole lot more interesting.

Someone had wanted Sizemore silenced, but why?

Cam needed to find out who had made those monthly calls from the prepaid phones, and he needed to find out what Lily had overheard the night her sister died.

The timing of Nicole's death and Gladys Sizemore's murder had just become a bit too convenient.

"Where are you?" Vince asked.

"With our favorite grieving relative."

Silence beat across the line.

"Vince?"

"For once in my life, pal, I don't know what to tell you."

"How about good luck."

"Good luck," Vince said before they ended the call.

But Cam had heard the uncertainty in his partner's voice. Just like Cam, Vince hadn't been sure of whether or not Cam was asking for good luck with the investigation, or with Lily.

As he stepped back into the case room, Lily lifted her focus to his. "Anything yet on the other person in the photo?" he asked.

"Male," Rick answered. "Appears to be fifteen or sixteen years old."

"Nothing else?"

"Not yet." Cam couldn't help but note the hint of defensiveness in Martin's voice. He wanted to prove himself, and wanted to prove himself badly.

Cam nodded, clearing his throat. "We had a new development."

Four pairs of eyes focused on him as he continued. "Apparently Gladys Sizemore didn't commit suicide. Coroner found an injection site at the base of her hairline."

"Could be insulin," Rick said, his suspicions paralleling Cam's.

"Won't know for four days."

"What about the empty pill bottle?" Lily asked.

"Probably for show. Killer might have flushed them for all we know."

The group fell silent, with one exception. A low rumble started in Trouble's throat, growing to a full-out growl as if he were trying to tell them something.

Cam turned his focus on Lily. "We need to know what you heard the night your sister died."

Her expression shifted from one of surprise to trepidation to determination. "Distortion. I wish I could remember more."

"Hypnosis." Kyle's voice surprised Cam, surprised everyone.

"Hypnosis?" Lily asked.

Silvia pushed away the quilt on which she'd been working and took Lily's hand.

"Do you believe you can be hypnotized?" the older woman asked, excitement shimmering in her pale eyes.

Lily took in a deep breath, then blew it out. "I'm not sure. I have to be honest with you."

Silvia leaned close and cupped Lily's cheek. "Do you trust me?"

"Of course." Lily spoke the words in a rush, covering Silvia's hand with her own.

Silvia smiled. "Then there's nothing to be worried about."

LILY HAD HEARD SILVIA HAD an interest in hypnosis, yet she'd never seen the woman in action. As she sat in a comfortable chair, eyes closed, doing her best to relax, she wondered what Cam thought of the scene playing out before him.

A team of rogue investigators engaging in mumbo jumbo in order to propel the case forward.

A laugh burst from her lips and Silvia sighed.

Lily snapped open her eyes and spotted the hurt on Silvia's face. "I'm not laughing at you. I'm laughing at what he must be thinking."

"Who?" Silvia scowled.

"Him," Lily said softly, pointing toward Cam. To her surprise, he sat on the edge of his seat, his body language fully engaged, not closed-off in the least.

He narrowed his eyes at her and Lily sank back into her seat, shutting her eyes again, rolling her shoulders to relax.

Silvia launched into a soothing patter, repeating phrases over and over, urging Lily to relax, to surrender her imagination.

A sense of weightlessness filled Lily, lifting away the heartache, the grief and the shock of the past several days. She felt more relaxed than she had in years and for a fleeting moment she wondered if she could stay like this forever.

"Do you remember the phone call, Lily?" Silvia asked.

Lily nodded, working to speak, but finding moving her mouth difficult at that moment.

"Take your time, dear." Silvia's soothing words flowed over her. "You're in complete control. Just concentrate on relaxing. Concentrate on letting your mind remember exactly what you heard."

"So many noises." Lily pushed the words through her lips.

"Turn them down," Silvia instructed. "Think of the voice analyzer back in Seattle and isolate the voice."

Words. Incoherent, but there. Behind the distortion. A deep, muffled voice.

"I think it's a man," Lily said, hearing the surprise in her own tone.

"Excellent." Silvia's voice grew louder, blending with the sounds in Lily's head as if she'd become hyper-aware of Silvia while everything else had fallen away—the other team members, Cam, her own heartbeat.

She heard only Silvia. Only Silvia and the man's voice, growing louder. Sharper.

"'Biggest headline of your career.'" Shock filled her as she spoke the words. How could she not have heard them before? Not have remembered them before? They were clear. *Clear.*

So was the sound of Nicole's struggle. Grunting. Kicking. Shuffling.

A tear slid down Lily's cheek and a heaviness pushed against her skull as if trying to get out.

"We can stop anytime." Silvia took Lily's hand, cradling it in her own. "Are you all right?"

"I hear them." Lily's voice cracked as she spoke. "I hear them," she whispered.

"Who, honey? Tell me who."

"They're struggling. Shuffling. 'Pity you won't be alive to see it.'"

"Who won't be alive?"

"Nicole." The pressure inside Lily's skull bordered on unbearable, but she had to hear the voice. Had to listen more carefully. She knew him. She'd spoken to him before. Had they met?

"Who's talking, Lily? Who's talking?"

"A man."

Conscious thought pushed at her hypnotic state, threatening to break through. Why? Was she too weak to handle the shock? Too weak to withstand the pain?

She could handle this, she could. Had she blocked the voice all this time to protect herself?

"Focus on the voice, Lily." Silvia squeezed her hand. "You're tensing up. Try to relax."

But she couldn't relax. Not a moment longer. Lily knew the voice. She knew whoever it was that had snuffed out her sister's life.

But who?

The pressure inside her skull intensified until she cried out.

"You'll wake up now," Silvia said. "On the count of three. One. Two. Three."

Lily blinked her eyes open, fully aware of her surroundings, free of pain, yet cognizant of what she'd said. "I know his voice."

"Maybe just from that call?" Rick asked.

But Lily shook her head, slowly, with purpose. "I've spoken to him, or I've heard him speak."

"Buddy Grey?" Cam asked.

Lily shook her head again. "I don't think I've ever heard him talk."

Rick raised a brow. "We've probably all heard him talk at some point or another. The man's given countless interviews proclaiming his innocence."

Rick was right, of course, but how could they be sure? "Do we have him on tape?" she asked.

"No." Martin pulled his chair tight to one of the computer stations, pulling up the Internet browser to launch a public video site. "But I can probably find him so fast your head will spin."

Lily wasn't sure how much more head spinning she could handle in one night.

Martin hit on a recent interview within seconds, the

segment credited to Nicole's news station. The piece started with a close-up of Grey, discussing how thrilled he was to be exonerated.

Lily didn't recognize the voice, but she did recognize something else about the man. There was something about him that was hauntingly familiar, yet just out of her reach.

His eyes? His nose?

What was it?

Her thoughts shattered the moment the camera panned back to Grey's interviewer.

Nicole's face filled the screen, her sleek brown hair, her carefully made up features, the soft, but firm lilt of her television voice—as the family had always called it.

A sob caught in Lily's throat and this time she didn't fight it. She slapped a hand over her mouth as she gasped, her vision swimming.

"Damn." Martin scrambled to minimize the image, to kill the sound. "I'm sorry. I wasn't thinking."

But Lily said nothing, only capable of focusing on two things.

Buddy Grey's voice was not the voice she'd heard on the phone.

And she was going to find her sister's killer and make him pay if it was the last thing she ever did.

CAM WATCHED LILY'S POSTURE change as they sat outside on the brownstone's small patio a short while later. She'd been visibly relaxed during Silvia's hypnosis, but that had changed rapidly once Nicole's image appeared on the computer screen.

Lily's pain had been so palpable Cam had wanted to slap the Off button himself.

Visibly shaken, she hadn't touched the meal Kyle had prepared for the team. Instead, she'd downed a cup of hot tea, nothing more.

The entire incident had served to reinforce Cam's need to focus on the case. He'd help Lily more by solving her sister's murder than he would by falling for her. But would he solve the murder more quickly by playing by police department protocol? Or would he uncover the truth more quickly utilizing the not-so-conventional methods of The Body Hunters?

As much as he hated to admit it, the covert band of operatives seemed to have a leg up in the effectiveness category.

As long as no evidence was mishandled, perhaps he was best to take a leave from the force just long enough to give him the freedom to work every angle of the case alongside Lily and her team.

His plan had the additional benefit of letting him keep Lily in his sights at all times—for protective purposes only, of course.

"Do you think your imagination conjured up the voice?" He asked the question tentatively, fully expecting an angry response.

"I wondered about that," Lily said instead. "I've read about hypnosis, and I knew about Silvia's skills, but I never dreamed she'd use them on me."

"So you're a skeptic?"

Lily tucked her knees up under her chin. "No. I've learned to believe anything's possible with this group."

She'd excused herself after losing her composure, seeking solitude in her room for a few moments. When she'd rejoined the team, she'd transformed back to a pair of jeans and a loose-fitting shirt. She'd changed her hair from the twist she'd worn to the funeral to a loose ponytail.

"I'd always wondered if a hypnotist could suggest something that would lead the responses given by the person hypnotized, but Silvia said nothing to plant that phrase in my head."

"Biggest headline of your career," Cam repeated. "Pity you won't be alive to see it." Lily winced and he apologized. "Sorry."

"Please—" she turned her chin toward him and forced a slight smile "—that's not as bad as seeing your sister alive and well."

"I'm sorry about that, too, in case I didn't say so before."

He reached for Lily's arm, but dropped his hand to his lap instead of making contact.

"Don't worry." She looked to the night sky and blew out a breath. "Poor Martin apologized enough for everyone."

"You're sure you're all right?"

She nodded.

"Because there is something we need to take care of."

"What?" She dropped her gaze back to Cam and the spark of life there relieved him a bit, reminded him that Lily was a strong woman who would survive this horrible ordeal.

"We need to see what's on that flash drive you found."

Lily sprang from the chair. "I forgot. How could I forget?"

Yet a few moments later as they huddled together over a laptop screen, Lily's tone had changed from one of disgust with herself to one of disgust with the flash drive.

"There's nothing here that I hadn't found on her virtual storage."

"Are you sure?" Cam asked.

Lily scanned the list of file folders again, trailing her finger down the screen. "Nothing."

"What about another type of folder, something other than a document."

Lily clicked a series of keys and a new screen appeared. "You're not too shabby with this detective stuff, Detective."

An odd warmth sprang to life in Cam's chest, although he did his best to ignore it. "Just doing my job."

She shot him a sideways glance. "So you keep telling me."

She pointed to the list on the screen. "Appointments. Three with Gladys Sizemore, one with someone named Nance and one at city hall."

"City hall?"

Lily bit down on her lip before she answered, squinting. "I don't think that's anything. Ross Patterson told me she'd planned a series of profiles on the upcoming election. He'd been looking forward to working with her."

Her voice trailed off on the last few words.

"What about the other name?" Maybe a shift in focus would ease the pained look on Lily's face. "Barbara Nance."

"Never heard of her." Lily opened her Internet browser and searched on all Barbara Nances in the state. She had one hit, not five miles from the old Camp Providence location.

"Looks like we've got a second stop to make tomorrow." Cam pushed to his feet. "You ready to turn in? We've got a long day ahead of us."

Lily nodded.

A second, unspoken question hung in the air between them as Cam turned toward the hall.

"I shouldn't have kissed you earlier." He hesitated at the doorway. "I apologize. I'm not sure what came over me." *Other than the relief of finding you safe.*

He continued without meeting Lily's gaze. "And don't

worry, I'll stay on the cot tonight no matter how cold you look."

Hours later, he watched Lily sleep, thinking about how relaxed she had appeared during hypnosis. She'd looked almost...happy.

He realized then that making her happy had become important to him. That and keeping her safe.

Cam held his ground through the night, never moving from the cot. He willed himself to fall asleep, knowing Lily had suffered enough heartache for one lifetime. She deserved someone better than him, someone who could give her the one thing she deserved.

Love.

Cam might want to hold her, talk to her, make love to her, but *love* her? He wouldn't know where to begin, what to say, how to act.

He hadn't loved anyone in a very long time with the exception of his daughter, and even that relationship had fallen apart, thanks for the most part to his ex-wife's move across country.

Cam hunkered down, ignoring the growing kink in his neck and the ache in his chest. He wouldn't pursue Lily, no matter how much he wanted to.

He might not know a thing about love, but he knew she'd thank him one day for walking out of her life, and he would walk out of her life.

That much he was sure of.

Chapter Eleven

Cam and Lily's trip to the Providence Mill's police department proved to be fruitless. Not only had the evidence box been lost years earlier, the logbook had gone missing as well. If the side trip to the Nance residence turned out to be equally worthless, today's round-trip drive would eat up six hours for nothing.

What a colossal waste of time.

Lily navigated while Cam drove toward the Nance home. The woman lived in the heart of a quaint historic area, surrounded by gift shops, cozy restaurants and hole-in-the-wall tourist haunts.

"Lovely," Lily said as he navigated the narrow streets.

"Sure," Cam answered. "If you're fond of running over tourists."

She rolled her eyes, although she had to admit she'd grown rather fond of Cam's surliness. She'd also come to realize most of the man's tough exterior was nothing more than an act.

She'd caught him watching her last night. For a brief

moment, she'd been tempted to invite him onto the bed. Not into the bed…but onto it. He'd looked so uncomfortable on the flimsy cot.

She'd resisted though, and her reluctance hadn't been because she didn't trust Cam. Truth was, Lily didn't trust herself. Her attraction to the dark-haired detective had steadily grown during the time she'd known him.

The kiss he'd planted on her back at Nicole's house hadn't done a thing to cool her interest. Far from it.

She glanced at the address for the Nance home and realized they were just about to drive past.

"There it is." She pointed.

Cam pulled the car into the drive and they headed straight for the front door without so much as planning their approach. They both knew what they wanted—any information they could find on the fateful summer Tracey Sizemore went missing.

A few minutes later, a very helpful Barbara Nance showed them the office of her late husband, Fred, the former manager of Camp Providence.

She'd offered them coffee, but both had declined, not wanting to intrude on the woman's privacy more than they already had.

"I was sorry to hear about your sister," she said to Lily. "She seemed so pleasant over the phone. Nothing like those other reporters you hear about who don't have time to really listen to people." Mrs. Nance's features twisted with genuine emotion. "She listened, your sister. I was looking forward to meeting her, even though she'd initially called looking for my husband."

"I'm sure she was looking forward to meeting you, as

well." Lily smiled broadly, doing her best to hide the heartache each mention of her sister's name caused.

How long would it last? The grief?

Lily wasn't sure she had it in her to take much more, although she knew she'd endure whatever lay in store for her. She was a Christides, after all.

"Well, I'm sorry for your loss," Mrs. Nance continued. "I lost my Fred over a year ago and I'm afraid it doesn't get much easier no matter how much time passes. At least not for me."

She graced Cam and Lily with a tight smile as she pushed open the door to a cluttered office. "As I told your sister when she called, Fred was a bit of a pack rat, but he was proud of his work. I can't bring myself to sort through his things. They meant so much to him." She clucked her tongue. "Never met a piece of paper he didn't like, that man. You're more than welcome to dig through, unless there's something specific you were after."

Lily and Cam exchanged doubtful glances. How would they ever find what they needed among the piles of accumulated material?

"Any idea of where he might have kept a list of camp attendees?" Cam asked.

Mrs. Nance's features instantly tightened. "He never was the same after that summer, you know." She waggled a finger at Lily. "That's what I told your sister. He never got over that young girl going missing on his watch."

"So, he was there that year?" Lily asked, hope blossoming inside her.

The older woman nodded as she worked her way through the maze of stacked file folders and archive boxes. "He didn't stay on much after that. Maybe a year or two.

He went downhill after he left, though. I supposed he missed the responsibility of running the camp."

Barbara Nance gripped a file box handle and hoisted the unwieldy object from the windowsill. "This one."

Cam crossed the room and lifted the weight of the visibly heavy item from Mrs. Nance's arms. "Do you mind if we flip through?"

Mrs. Nance shook her head, her eyes sad. "Detective, I don't mind if you take it. I need to face the fact Fred's gone and throw this mess out. No one cared about this paperwork except Fred."

"We care, Mrs. Nance." Lily reached for the woman's hand, taking it in her own. "Thank you."

CAM HAD CALLED LIEUTENANT Casey that morning and voluntarily removed himself from the case. He'd also requested the use of his accumulated vacation time.

He'd told himself Lily needed him, but the reality was the woman didn't need anyone.

She could more than hold her own—both at the police department and here, one on one with the widow Nance.

Lily's kind and sincere demeanor put the woman instantly at ease, something Cam could learn from. He'd never much worried about other people's feelings the way Lily did.

Her technique worked. Beautifully.

Each day he knew her, he found something new to admire, something new to think about, something new to learn from.

Perhaps if he stayed focused on the case, he wouldn't feel the void too sharply when Lily returned to Seattle.

He laughed to himself as he pulled into a restaurant parking lot.

"What?" Lily frowned at him from the passenger seat.

"Guy stuff." He purposely kept his tone gruff as he cut the ignition and climbed out of the car.

Lily muttered her thoughts under her breath and Cam stifled a grin. "Let's find the biggest table they've got, order a pot of coffee and spread out."

A few moments later, they were all set. Chalk one up to small-town hospitality.

They'd filled every available inch of the table with the unbelievable volume of paper Fred Nance had crammed into the filing container.

His wife had been correct, however. Most of the contents seemed to be either camper applications or attendee lists. Unfortunately, the paperwork spanned fifteen years of time, and had been filed in no particular order.

"This is going to take all day," Cam muttered in between sips of hot coffee and random passes through stacks of paperwork.

Lily pursed her lips and pinned him with a glare. "Think of it as an audit. Pick a pile and work it through. Don't waste time reading what's on the page." She tapped the corner of a sheet in front of her. "Find the date and move on. If it's not our year, we don't care what it says."

Cam sank back in his seat and shot her a look that had silenced plenty of suspects in his time. Lily, however, had already dropped her focus to her work and ignored him completely.

She had a point, as much as he hated to admit it. So he set to work, following Lily's method. His eyes had just begun to glaze over when Lily inhaled sharply.

"You found it?" He held out a hand.

Lily's mouth worked, but formed no words. Her brows

pulled together as she handed over the sheet, pointing toward the top of the page.

Cam scanned the paper, swearing softly when he spotted two very familiar names listed under the camp counselor section.

Timothy Fitzsimmons and Langston Montgomery. The head of Rebuild Philadelphia and the city's soon-to-be outgoing mayor.

"Oh." A hearty laugh escaped Cam, drawing the attention of nearby diners. "I am so going to enjoy this." He thought of Fitzsimmons in particular. What Cam wouldn't give to find that man dirty after all.

"It was a very popular camp back then." Lily leaned forward, reaching for the sheet.

"How long had your sister been dating Fitzsimmons?" Cam slid the paper back in Lily's direction, watching as she ran a finger down the length of names.

"Not long." She shook her head. "Maybe a few weeks. She didn't really talk much about him, so it must have been a new thing."

Cam's investigative gut kicked to life. "You don't see anything wrong with that?"

"Should I?" She studied his features closely.

"Your sister begins looking into the Sizemore case and Fitzsimmons suddenly asks her out. I wonder if he volunteered information about his time at camp, or whether he was more interested in getting close enough to Nicole to know exactly what she found out and when?"

The color drained from Lily's face. "In case he had something to hide?"

Cam pointed to the sheet of paper. "Exactly."

But Lily's attention had been absorbed by something else on the sheet. "Didn't Buddy Grey have a brother?"

Cam nodded, snatching the paper from her fingertips. "A younger brother. Bobby."

And there it was, in black and white. Bobby Grey. He'd been there when Tracey Sizemore had gone missing and while Fitzsimmons and Montgomery had worked as counselors.

Was there a connection to his brother, Buddy?

Things were heating up.

"Could be another Bobby Grey." But Lily's skeptical tone gave away her doubt.

She and Cam both knew they'd stumbled on to something big…at last.

Cam shuffled the piles of paper back together, cramming them into the file folder. "We need to get back to the city."

But when he looked at Lily, determination shimmered in her gaze. "Why don't you head back without me?"

Cam arched a brow.

"There's someone in New York State I need to visit."

He could read her mind as if she'd spoken the name out loud. "Dorothy Grey?" Buddy and Bobby's mother.

Lily nodded. "Can't be more than six hours from here."

"You take my car, I'll rent one and drive back."

Lily pulled out her cell phone. "That would slow you down too much. I can have a car here in no time."

"One of your team?"

"No." She keyed in a text message then shut the phone. "One of the team's contacts."

Cam didn't argue. He also didn't wait for Lily's car to arrive before he headed back to Philadelphia. He knew she didn't mind.

After all, they were on the same side now, he and Lily. And if Fitzsimmons or Montgomery had had a thing to do with either the Sizemore disappearance or Nicole's death, both he and Lily wanted the truth and a full confession yesterday.

They were closing in on the truth, and nothing could stop them now.

"WHAT EXACTLY IS IT YOU'RE trying to say, Detective Hughes? I've never known you to beat around the bush."

"And I've never known you to give a straight answer."

Cam paced a tight pattern in front of Tim Fitzsimmons's desk. Mayor Montgomery was in Harrisburg for the day, but Tim had been gracious enough to invite Cam into his office.

The expression he wore now suggested he more than regretted that particular decision.

Cam scanned Fitzsimmons's bookcase, chock-full of Lucite awards and sleek plaques, each engraved with words of congratulations and praise for the man's work to house the city's poor.

He studied the shelves, moving past the awards to zero in on the photographs.

Tim with the outgoing mayor.

Tim with the soon-to-be incoming mayor.

Tim with the President of the United States when Rebuild Philadelphia had been named a model for the nation.

This was how Cam knew Tim best. The man loved his notoriety, probably far more than he loved those he served.

Tim Fitzsimmons craved the photographer's flash. Cam wondered how far he'd go to make sure nothing—and no one—threatened the powerful position he'd worked so hard for.

Cam spun on one heel, visibly surprising Tim with the

sudden move. "Did you pursue her romantically in order to keep tabs on her?"

Fitzsimmons's eyes narrowed to slits. "What in the hell are you talking about?"

"Nicole." Cam crossed to the man's desk and slammed his fist against the sleek, polished surface. "Did you date her to make sure she wouldn't hurt your career?"

"How on earth could she hurt my career?"

Cam tossed a copy of the Camp Providence registration list from that summer on top of the spotless—and empty—desk.

Cam wondered, and not for the first time, whether Fitzsimmons was merely a showpiece for the people in his administration who actually worked and gave a damn about the city's disadvantaged.

He kept that particular thought to himself as Tim reached for the paper. Cam waited and watched as the other man's gaze slid down the page.

This time when Tim snapped his focus up to meet Cam's, indignation wasn't the only emotion lurking in his cold glare. If Cam wasn't mistaken, Tim Fitzsimmons looked a bit shocked…and panicked.

"Did you know Tracey Sizemore? I understand they questioned each camper after she vanished." Cam leaned across the desk, so much so that Tim flinched. "What did you say when they questioned you, Fitzsimmons? Or did you neglect to tell the investigators something?

"Maybe you've kept a secret all these years? A secret Nicole unearthed working on her newest story? A secret that could jeopardize all of this?" Cam pointed to the shelves of awards and photos, to the walls filled with certificates, proclamations and news articles.

"You knew she'd met with Gladys Sizemore, didn't you? You found out somehow and you decided that now would be a good time to date Nicole. What happened?" Cam shrugged, turning back to face Fitzsimmons.

"How about Bobby Grey? I understand he was there that same year. Tell me—" Cam stepped back to the desk and braced his fists against the desktop "—was what Nicole uncovered really worth her dying?"

Fitzsimmons's cheeks had gone scarlet, his anger palpable and heavy in the air, even before he spoke.

"You don't know what the hell you're talking about. Or who you're dealing with." He jabbed a finger in Cam's face, "Be careful, Detective. Be very, very careful."

But he didn't wait around for Cam's response.

He rounded his desk, crossed the room and slammed his own office door behind him as he left.

Cam bit back a smile, filled with nothing but pure satisfaction.

When word of this got back to his lieutenant, the man would no doubt have his head, but Cam had definitely hit a nerve.

He stole another glance at the door and grinned just thinking about how much Lily would have enjoyed Fitzsimmons's little display of temper.

He'd hit a nerve, all right.

And based on the way Tim had stormed out of his own office, Cam had hit a big nerve.

Now Cam just had to figure out exactly what that nerve had been.

LILY STOOD ON THE FRONT STEP of Dorothy Grey's house and wondered if she'd made a huge mistake. An American flag hung from one of the porch roof's freshly painted columns and two pots of red impatiens framed the front door.

The well-kept house sent the signal that guests were welcome, yet Lily imagined Mrs. Grey might be more than a little surprised to find the sister of her son's most recent alleged victim on her front doorstep.

Lily rang the bell and the front door opened without so much as a question about who waited on the other side. City versus country, Lily thought.

Of course, the unmarked police cruiser parked across the street didn't hurt.

"Mrs. Grey?" Lily spoke tentatively, reigning in her usual blunt tone.

The older woman smiled. Her silver hair had been cut into a stylish pageboy, and a pair of turquoise glasses hung around her neck from a strand of colorful beads.

"Won't you come in?" Grey held the door wide.

Lily opened her mouth then closed it, then opened it again. "Aren't you going to ask who I am or why I'm here?"

"I know exactly why you're here." She gestured for Lily to step inside. "And who you are."

Lily blinked. "You do?"

Mrs. Grey nodded. "You think my Buddy killed your sister." She stepped aside to let Lily enter. "Coffee or tea, dear?"

Lily stepped inside, wondering momentarily if she'd entered the twilight zone. Mrs. Grey had accused Lily of thinking Buddy guilty, yet she'd invited her inside just the same.

"I actually don't think your son killed my sister, Mrs. Grey."

"Then why are you here, dear?" This time when the woman met Lily's gaze, a coldness in her navy eyes sent a shiver down Lily's spine.

"I wanted to ask you about Bobby."

Mrs. Grey visibly flinched. "Bobby's been out of our lives for a long time."

"You've never heard from him?" Lily asked.

"Never." Grey paled for a moment, then gathered her composure. "How about some tea?"

Lily nodded, taken aback by Mrs. Grey's response to everything from her visit to her questions about her son. "Tea would be lovely. Can I help you at all?"

Grey gestured to a faded floral sofa. "Make yourself at home. I'll be right out."

Lily waited uncomfortably, oddly unnerved by Dorothy Grey's reactions, or should she say, lack of reactions.

Lily made a move to pass the time by doing the usual things one did while a guest in someone else's home. She looked around the cozy space for photos or knickknacks to admire, yet found none.

Dorothy Grey's living space was devoid of all personal touches home owners usually displayed.

Why? Lily wondered. Too painful? Too harsh a reminder of one son on the wrong side of the law and the other son gone?

She waited until Grey had set a tea service and a plate of cookies on the coffee table before she spoke again.

"I don't mean to press the point, ma'am, but your son disappeared nineteen years ago. You've never had any communication from him?"

For a split second, Lily thought she spotted a shadow of sadness in Grey's eyes. "The police were sure he'd run away. He left a note, actually. Said he wanted no parts of our name or family."

She fixed her moisture-filled gaze on Lily. "If it hadn't been for Buddy, I'm not sure I would have survived that. But Buddy…Buddy was always my good boy."

"Bobby was younger?"

Grey nodded, tipping the teapot to fill two pristine china cups. "He was, yes."

"Do you ever wonder where he is?"

The other woman shook her head. "He's gone, dear. Do you have any children?"

Lily shook her head.

"Sometimes you just have to let go," Grey continued. "And I had my Buddy."

"I wonder if you might have a picture somewhere?"

"Of Bobby?" Grey frowned slightly.

Lily nodded.

"I do." Grey answered in the affirmative, but made no move to retrieve a photo, or anything else, for that matter.

Lily decided not to press that point.

The two women sat quietly for several uncomfortable moments while Lily found herself suffering from an uncharacteristic loss for words.

Here she sat across from a woman resigned to the fact one son had vanished and in denial over the fact the other son—recently freed on a triple-murder charge, no less—was once again a wanted man.

"Have you heard from Buddy?" she asked, hoping she hadn't made a tactical error.

Grey smiled and gave a quick shrug. "Buddy will reach out to me when things die down." She lifted a cookie from the plate and waved it toward the window. "I'm sure you spotted the police car outside."

Lily nodded.

"My Buddy's too smart to call or stop by right now." She took a bite of cookie then chewed and swallowed before she continued. "I understand. Poor thing. Everyone's always thought him guilty, when truth was, he's never been anything but innocent."

She pushed the plate of cookies toward Lily. "Go ahead, dear. They're sugar free. Quite tasty."

Sugar free? Lily thought of the injection mark on the back of Gladys Sizemore's neck and the possible use of insulin as a murder weapon.

"Are you diabetic?" she asked nonchalantly.

Dorothy Grey nodded. "Oh my, yes. Runs through the whole family. Even my Buddy."

Lily bit back her excitement.

Had Buddy Grey killed Gladys Sizemore? But why?

Had Nicole made some connection between the Grey boys and Tracey Sizemore? Something she'd told Buddy about? Something that had gotten both Nicole and Sizemore killed?

Dorothy Grey pushed to her feet and opened a cabinet, sliding out a photo album of some sort. "Here. I showed this to your sister when she was here."

Lily forced her head back into the moment, lowering her teacup before she took the album from Mrs. Grey's hands.

She gently opened the cover, realizing the album had some age on it. "How old is this?"

"Why, twenty-one years, I believe. He saved the dates with the newspaper articles."

Dates? Newspaper articles?

Lily turned the first page, then the second, scanning the collection of faded newspaper clippings and photographs.

Her blood ran cold.

"Was this Buddy's?" She forced the question through a tight throat.

Mrs. Grey smiled brightly. "You see? My Buddy would never hurt a fly." She leaned toward Lily and ran a finger across one of the pages, almost lovingly. "He was so upset when his friend Claire vanished and then devastated when they found her body. He saved every scrap of news. I'll never forget it."

Her features twisted with genuine emotion. "He was horrified by what someone had done to that girl. How anyone could ever accuse him of a crime is beyond me."

The urge to drop the book and scrub her hands overcame Lily.

Horrified?

The collection of saved newspaper articles and photographs apparently cut from missing flyers was anything *but* a display of how horrified Buddy Grey had been by Claire Mooney's death.

If anything, the album solidified the fact the man was a cold-blooded killer who had started his crime spree even earlier than the police suspected, based on the dates of these clippings.

Some killers loved keepsakes.

Lily had seen enough during her time with The Body Hunters to learn that much. Buddy Grey had obviously cherished every word printed about his first kill.

Claire Mooney. A young girl whose murder had apparently gone unsolved.

A cold chill slid across Lily's shoulders. "You said my sister saw this?"

"Oh, yes." Dorothy Grey nodded vigorously. "She poured over it just like you. Every word."

Lily's heart fell to her stomach. "When was that, Mrs. Grey?" She dreaded the answer even as she asked the question.

"When she first came to see me, not long after she started profiling Buddy's fight for acquittal on the nightly news."

So Nicole had seen this and had still fought for Grey's freedom. She'd seen this and she'd surely known exactly what Lily knew now.

The man was a cold-blooded killer.

And yet, Nicole had pursued his acquittal. She'd pursued the story. Pursued her career-making exclusive.

Lily's stomach flipped. "Might I use your rest room?"

A moment later, she stared at her reflection, taken aback by the hollow set of her grief-rimmed eyes. She turned on the cold spigot and cupped a handful of water, splashing her face over and over again until the wave of nausea left her.

Cam had been right.

Nicole had knowingly worked to free a guilty man.

She'd cared more about her career than about keeping a killer behind bars.

Chances were pretty good she'd paid for her actions with her life.

Lily gathered herself, dried her face and, armed with one last question, headed back toward where Dorothy Grey waited. "Mrs. Grey?"

"Yes, dear?"

"Did Buddy know you'd shown his keepsake album to my sister?"

"Of course, dear. I tell Buddy everything."

I tell Buddy everything.

The words haunted Lily as she thought about Nicole's death, Gladys Sizemore's death, all of it. Both cases. Both puzzles. Somehow connected. Lily knew it in her heart.

A few moments later, Lily pulled away from the curb in front of the Grey home, but not before Mrs. Grey had given her something to take with her. A faded school photograph of Bobby Grey, more than twenty years old, she'd explained.

Lily gave a short wave to the two officers working surveillance. She might have something concrete on Bobby, but she'd walked away without anything but supposition on Buddy. What she wouldn't have given to turn his keepsake album over to the team.

Claire Mooney. Buddy Grey's first kill.

If Buddy Grey knew Nicole had seen the album, he'd know the reporter had access to potential evidence in a case as yet untried. A case that could send him back to jail.

I tell Buddy everything.

Dorothy Grey's words continued to ring in Lily's ears.

Mrs. Grey might not have spoken to Buddy yet, but when she did, she'd no doubt brag about how another Christides sister had admired his keepsakes.

And then Lily would become Buddy's next target.

She thought of Nicole's missing cell phone and the call Lily had placed to that number.

For all Lily knew, she was already Buddy Grey's next target. After all, if the man had Nicole's phone, he had only to read the log of incoming calls to know exactly whose call had connected in the moments before Nicole's death.

How foolish had Lily been to believe the man's methods had been copied to deflect guilt from someone else.

Buddy Grey had obviously killed Nicole, and if he'd killed that quickly after his release from prison, he wouldn't hesitate to kill again.

She blew out a sigh and glanced at a highway mileage sign as she passed.

Three-hundred and seventy miles to go before she was back in Philadelphia. Back with the team. Back with Cam.

But where was Buddy Grey?

What if he'd killed Tracey Sizemore all those years ago while visiting his brother at camp? What if he'd killed his own brother?

Her sister had let loose a monster—a monster with no soul. And for what? A story? A promotion?

"Damn you, Nicole."

The grief that had gripped her for days slowly relinquished its hold, edged out by the anger simmering to life inside Lily's belly.

She'd use the next rest stop to put in a call to Cam and the team.

In the meantime, Buddy Grey was out there somewhere.

And Lily's efforts had just cemented the target on her own back.

Oh well—she sighed—she had three-hundred and seventy miles to get used to the idea.

TIM FITZSIMMONS STOOD with his back to the path, clad in running shorts, sneakers and a warm-up jacket. The early summer night was cool, moonless and Fitzsimmons tapped one foot as he checked his watch.

Fitzsimmons had never been the sharpest of the bunch,

but his good looks and connections had carried him far, straight to the head of Rebuild Philadelphia.

Well, The Man chuckled inwardly, that ride was about to end.

According to the panicked call The Man had received from Fitzsimmons, Detective Hughes had bandied about some interesting theories, including the idea Tim had pursued Nicole simply to keep an eye on her interest in the Sizemore case.

Bravo, Detective Hughes.

The Man stepped closer, silently, raising the hand that held his weapon.

Fitzsimmons apparently didn't hear a thing above the noise filtering over the expressway that sliced down the middle of Fairmount Park.

The Man lined up the muzzle of the gun to the back of Fitzsimmons's perfectly coiffed head. He tried to feel something for the person he'd known for years, but oddly he couldn't muster a single emotion or reason to spare this particular life.

The most disappointing aspect of the entire situation was that Fitzsimmons wouldn't feel a thing.

Pity.

The Man squeezed off a single shot and Fitzsimmons crumpled in a heap.

The Man didn't waste his time checking for a pulse. The shot had been instantly fatal. Another soul lost. Another weak link successfully eliminated.

He'd deposit the gun in the Schuylkill River after he left the park. Perhaps he'd even stop for a drink to celebrate.

He killed out of necessity, yes, but he enjoyed the power just the same as if he'd killed for pleasure.

He should have thanked Fitzsimmons before he killed him. After all, he'd given The Man a reason to eliminate another threat. Make that two threats.

Apparently Cameron Hughes and Lily Christides made quite an investigative team—an investigative team that was getting far too close to the truth.

The time had come to eliminate the detective and the overly curious sister.

And The Man knew just how to do so.

Chapter Twelve

Body Clock: 109:05

"I always said jogging wasn't good for anyone." Vince sipped from his foam coffee cup before he turned and walked away, leaving Cam staring down at the very lifeless body of Tim Fitzsimmons.

The sun had barely risen when an early-morning jogger called in the discovery of a John Doe in Fairmount Park. The victim hadn't remained a John Doe for long, not with one of the most photographed faces in the city.

Obviously Cam had hit a bigger nerve than he'd thought.

"Hughes." Lieutenant Casey's voice sliced through the otherwise subdued scene.

"Yes, sir." Cam turned to face the music, and he knew there'd be music. You didn't grill a top level city official while supposedly out on vacation and not end up taking an earful, if not worse.

Considering that same top level city official had apparently been shot execution style, a suspension would probably be the least of Cam's worries.

But instead of giving Cam an earful, Casey pulled up

short, directing his next question at Vince and his temporary partner. "What have you got?"

"Timothy Fitzsimmons. Aged thirty-six. Apparently shot at close range."

"Drugs?"

"Not that we've found."

"Enemies?"

A sharp burst of laughter slid between Cam's lips. "Sorry sir," he mumbled.

Casey turned on him then. "For a man who's supposed to be on vacation, you sure got an early start this morning. Out for a walk?"

"Something like that." Cam dropped his gaze to the body, knowing he was treading on very thin ice.

"Be careful, Detective," Casey continued. "As I understand the facts, you may be the last person to see Fitzsimmons alive. Some hotshot lawyer will have a field day with that."

So the lieutenant knew about Cam's visit to city hall. Word traveled fast.

Cam shot a glare at Vince who arched a brow and gave Cam the signal to shut up.

Cam ignored him. "I felt Fitzsimmons might have information critical to the Christides investigation, sir."

"The investigation on which you are no longer involved?"

Cam winced. "Yes, sir."

"And did he?"

"I was working on warming him up, sir."

"Warming him up?" This time when Casey spoke, his tone left no room for misunderstanding. Cam had screwed up royally.

"According to Fitzsimmons's secretary, you provoked

her boss and angered him to such an extent that he stormed out of his own office." Casey leaned so close Cam could guess the brand of mouthwash the man had used before he left the house that morning.

Cam reached for his pocket, swearing slightly when he found it empty of even the lousy gum he chewed.

"Tread carefully, Hughes. I don't suffer fools lightly."

"Understood, sir." Cam stepped back from the scene, playing the role of dutiful detective.

"I suggest you leave this scene up to those members of the response team who aren't on vacation, while you head downtown to file a report on your little talk with Fitzsimmons."

Before Cam could say a word or make a move to defend his actions, Casey was gone, leaving Cam with only one thing to do. Find Lily and The Body Hunters as fast as he could.

The report could wait.

Lily had called him during the night, filling him in on her meeting with Dorothy Grey.

Cam hadn't thought things could get much more interesting.

How wrong he'd been.

But, he wasn't wrong about the technology in The Body Hunters' case room. They'd no doubt be able to access information that might take Cam days of paperwork and requisitions. Days he didn't have.

There were times when there was much to be said for not playing by the rules.

This was one of those times.

He needed Fitzsimmons's phone logs. Every single one.

If the now-dead director of Rebuild Philadelphia had

placed a call last night, Cam wanted to know to whom and when.

He was becoming increasingly convinced Lily had been right all along. Her sister had stumbled upon something that had gotten her killed, and the body count was rising.

Cam intended to stop the killer in his tracks before he struck again. And if that meant throwing out the rules, so be it.

CAM JOINED THE TEAM just as they began their latest briefing. Lily warmed at the sight of him, glad to have him in the room.

She'd driven straight through from the Grey home and had grabbed a few hours of sleep, not much more. Adrenaline was an amazing thing. She didn't want to think about how hard she was going to crash whenever it wore off, though.

"Was it Tim?" she asked, realizing instantly where Cam had been.

He nodded. "Single bullet. Back of the skull."

She winced, picturing the man her sister had briefly dated.

"Can we pull his phone records?" Cam pulled a chair to the table, joining the rest of the team as if he'd always been a part of the group.

It struck Lily then how well he fit. She shoved the thought away. Whenever this case ended, the team—Lily included—would return to Seattle. Cam would stay behind. For all intents and purposes, she'd probably never see the man again.

Silvia opened a laptop and tapped a series of keys. A listing of phone numbers, dates and times appeared on the projection screen.

"Ask and you shall receive."

Cam grinned and shook his head. "When did you do this?"

"The second the story broke." Silvia beamed proudly. "You interested in any feature in particular?"

Cam stood and studied the screen. "Two things. Any calls to or from any of our prepaid numbers."

Silvia clucked her tongue. "Already checked. No hits."

"Damn," Cam muttered. "How about any calls made after I saw him yesterday."

"Time?" Silvia asked, leaning into her keyboard.

"About three-thirty, four o'clock."

Silvia hit the keys and a section of the screen enlarged, highlighting a single call made from Fitzsimmons's home phone at five o'clock. A second screen opened, searching for a hit on the receiving number.

The search spit back one name and the murmurs from the other team members matched Cam's thoughts exactly.

Sonofa—

"Mayor Montgomery." Lily read the name without emotion.

"They were already pulling him in for questioning," Cam explained. "I gave them a copy of the camp list."

With that, his cell rang. He excused himself and stepped into the hall.

"There's still a big piece here that hasn't been explained." Rick stood and paced a tight pattern in the small room.

"The prepaid phones?" Kyle asked.

Rick nodded. "Exactly."

Cam stepped back into the room, his expression tense. "I have to head to the precinct."

Lily pushed to her feet, frightened by his expression. "What is it?"

"Montgomery's about to turn himself in."

"Mayor Montgomery?" Lily asked. "For Tim?"

Cam shook his head. "For Sizemore. *Tracey* Sizemore."

Lily sank back into her chair. Could the Sizemore mystery be over? Just like that?

"I'll call you as soon as I know more." Cam turned to leave.

"In the meantime we'll divide the city, hit every retail location for the prepaid phone providers used." Rick crossed to Cam and patted his shoulder. "Keep us posted on Montgomery."

Lily recognized the move. Rick now considered Cam a friend, they all did. He'd become one of them.

"Will do." Cam hesitated on his way out the door, pinning Lily with a quick look. "I'll get back when I can."

"We're fine." But she knew it wasn't the rest of the team to whom he'd been talking. As much as the independent woman inside her had initially fought the notion, he wasn't such a bad guy to have around.

She might as well enjoy Cam's attention while it lasted.

At the rate things were going, she'd be back to life in Seattle before she knew it, leaving Detective Hughes far, far behind.

Cam stopped again, throwing one last question at the group. "Anything on Bobby Grey?"

"Nothing," Silvia answered. "The kid might as well have fallen off the face of the earth."

"Maybe he did just that."

CAM READ MONTGOMERY'S body language through the interrogation room's two-way mirror. Hours had passed since he first showed up at the station, and even then Montgomery had appeared later than originally planned.

Apparently a confession by the incumbent mayor was a bit more complicated than your average confession.

Additionally, Cam had passed Vince the information on the series of calls to Gladys Sizemore's home prior to her death. The team of investigators had first validated the information and had then secured Montgomery's approval to search his office.

The man had sworn he had nothing to hide, but the station was abuzz with information to the contrary.

The media frenzy outside the precinct was like none Cam had witnessed during his time on the force. At last count, every regional station was represented, as well as network talking heads from up and down the East Coast.

Cam had spoken with Lily twice. The team had found nothing in their efforts to identify the purchaser of the prepaid phones. With any luck at all, that mystery was about to be solved.

Daylight had begun to pale outside the windows when Montgomery's questioning finally began.

Lieutenant Casey had agreed to let Cam watch the man's confession on Cam's word that he'd keep his mouth shut and remain uninvolved.

Cam wasn't sure he could deliver, but he'd made the deal. And right now, looking at the guilt on Montgomery's face, any concession Cam made had been worth it to see the mighty fall.

Oddly enough, Montgomery looked more relaxed than he had during his entire career in Philadelphia politics.

Maybe the nightmare of holding on to his secret for the past nineteen years had taken a toll far greater than what he'd expected.

His close-cropped hair appeared mussed, as if he'd been running his fingers through it. His pale-blue eyes, typically tense and controlled, appeared resigned.

The news of his involvement in the Sizemore disappearance had stunned the police department. Apparently, Tim's murder had been the impetus for the man's change of heart. The time had come to end the charade.

"Do you have any idea who might have shot Mr. Fitzsimmons?" The interrogation officer kicked back in his chair, working to give the appearance of a friend asking questions, not an officer of the law ready to document Montgomery's crime.

Montgomery hesitated for a split second before he answered. "No."

"You see that?" Excitement filtered through Vince's voice as he leaned close to the two-way mirror.

Cam nodded, having spotted the move.

"Another random shooting in a city sadly known for its murder rate," the mayor continued.

But Cam wasn't buying it. Based on the look on the interrogation officer's face, he wasn't buying Montgomery's line, either, but he moved past the resistance, focusing on the sure bet.

The confession.

"Why don't you tell me exactly what happened nineteen years ago at Camp Providence?"

Montgomery took a sip of water, then closed his eyes as if he had to work to conjure up the memories. The pained expression on his face suggested he'd never forgotten a detail.

"I liked her." Montgomery blew out a sigh. "Counselors weren't allowed to fraternize with the campers, but we did. We all did. She was younger."

He shoved a hand through his hair, the move in direct opposition to the stiff control he'd shown in public for as long as Cam could remember. "I asked her to walk with me, and Tim came along as my lookout."

"Did she know that?" the interrogation officer asked.

Montgomery shook his head. "She probably thought she was safer with the two of us." He laughed, the sound bitter and defeated. "When she rejected my kiss, I pushed her. I never meant for her to fall." Another hand through his hair. "I sound like a cliché."

"Did she die instantly?"

Montgomery paled, his eyes going vacant. "I think so. She went still instantly, and I yelled for Tim."

"But neither of you went for help?"

The mayor shook his head. "She wasn't moving. She'd hit her head. What good would help have done?" He held up a hand as if he knew how stupid he sounded now. "We were kids. We were stupid. And we both had scholarships to top universities that would vanish once word got out about what had happened."

Selfish bastard, Cam thought.

"So you left her there?" The officer leaned forward.

Montgomery nodded. "We moved her to a gully, figured she was already dead and everyone would think she'd run away or gotten lost."

"What if a search party found her?"

"They never did."

The interviewer merely widened his gaze.

"We made it look like she'd fallen accidentally."

"You posed her?"

Montgomery closed his eyes and nodded.

"I need a verbal response."

The mayor took another sip of water, then spoke, his voice tight with emotion and guilt. "We posed her."

The interrogation officer stood and paced a tight pattern next to the table. "Why not lie and say you'd found her that way?"

Another hesitation. "We were stupid. We panicked." He breathed in sharply. "We never wanted to see her again."

Yet Gladys Sizemore had spent the rest of her days searching for her niece. Cam fought the urge to pound his fists against the glass.

"Mayor Montgomery, where were you last Saturday night?"

"Home with my wife."

"Have you ever spoken with a Gladys Sizemore, Tracey's aunt?"

Montgomery's forehead crumpled. "I have not. No."

"What would you say if I told you that today's search of your office resulted in the discovery of a prepaid cell phone matching that used to call Gladys Sizemore on two occasions during this past month? The last being during the hours before she died?"

Montgomery blinked but said nothing.

"Your home records indicate that Mr. Fitzsimmons called you not long before he was shot. What did you two speak about?"

"He was upset about something."

Cam's little visit to his office, no doubt.

"Did you kill him?" the interrogation officer continued.

Angry blotches fired in Montgomery's face. "No, I didn't kill him. He was my friend. His death is the reason I came forward."

"Why come forward if the only witness to your crime is dead?"

Montgomery fell silent, splaying his hands flat on the

table. "I think we're done here." Montgomery pushed to his feet, and beside him, his attorney stood. "I was involved in the accidental death of Tracey Sizemore nineteen years ago. I have been involved in no additional crimes. I came forward today so that Tracey Sizemore's memory can be laid to rest."

"So says he," Vince muttered softly, his face inches from the glass of the two-way mirror. He turned to Cam as Montgomery and his lawyer were led out of the room. "What do you think?"

"I think he's not telling the full story."

"You like him for the Sizemore murder?"

Cam shook his head. "I can't see him sticking a needle in her neck, can you?"

"No." Vince leaned his back against the glass. "Why let us search his office if he knew the phone was there?"

Cam turned to leave. "Maybe he didn't know it was there."

"A third party?"

Cam shrugged, his brain on overdrive.

"What about Fitzsimmons?" Vince's question trailed Cam out the door.

"I don't think he shot himself in the back of the head."

He headed for the door, wanting to get to Lily. Against his wishes, she'd gone to her parents' shop after hours.

He'd planned on meeting her there, but at this rate, he'd be at least an hour late.

"You'll call me if anything changes?"

Vince nodded as Cam headed back out into the muggy Philadelphia night air, hurrying toward his car.

Tonight of all nights, he didn't like the idea of Lily being alone.

Chapter Thirteen

Lily sat at the small metal desk at the back of her parents' dry cleaning shop and groaned at the mess her father had made of the store's financial record keeping.

Cam had phoned her to say he was running late. She assured him she was fine. After all, she had Trouble with her. What could happen?

Apparently a search of the mayor's office had turned up one of the prepaid cell phones The Body Hunters had spent the entire day trying to track down.

They'd canvassed the city, retail outlet by retail outlet, showing three pictures. Buddy Grey. Tim Fitzsimmons. Langston Montgomery.

While most clerks recognized the faces from recent news, none remembered selling a prepaid phone to any of them.

And so they'd ended the day with a big fat nothing in the way of progress.

Until Cam's call.

The theory was that Montgomery had killed Gladys Sizemore just as he'd killed her niece years earlier. It all seemed so senseless, though, the snowballing of an accident into reason for multiple murders and lives ruined.

Lily could tell from Cam's voice that he wasn't sold on the theory of Montgomery's guilt in Gladys Sizemore's death. Maybe that's what made him so good at his work. He never stopped questioning.

Lily's stomach caught and twisted at the thought of the detective. The man had wreaked havoc on her senses.

While she'd always admired her parents' love for each other and their closeness, Lily had never experienced a romantic entanglement that didn't end up with a broken heart—hers. And she'd never much cared for broken hearts.

When the time came to return to Seattle, she realized it would be the memory of Cam's face, the memory of his touch, that would keep her up at night.

As for the detective, his feelings on romance were plain to see. He'd been hurt once, and missed his daughter terribly, even if he'd never admitted as much to her. Surely he had no plans to risk his heart again.

She blew out a deep sigh and studied the dry cleaning shop. She'd spent most of her childhood here, after school and on weekends. While Nicole had complained about being cooped up, Lily had enjoyed playing bookkeeper. Once she'd been old enough to master the math, she'd actually taken over.

She glanced down at her father's ledger and clucked her tongue. Good thing she'd stopped by. He'd made a mess of his monthly receipts…as usual.

A noise sounded from somewhere deep inside the shop and Trouble growled. The terrier had been asleep at her feet, his chin resting on top of her foot.

"Nothing to worry about, boy." She reached down and gave him a scratch between the ears.

She supposed the monstrous machinery and the shadows they cast would appear a bit intimidating to anyone not used to them, especially with only the desk lamp and few night lights on around the space.

Shadows stretched from one side of the shop to the other, diffused only by the subtle glow of the streetlamp outside shining through the plate glass window in front.

Something crashed at the back of the shop and this time Lily sat to attention even more quickly than Trouble did.

That was not a sound that belonged in the shop.

"Hello?" She pushed back her chair and stood. "Dad?" Maybe her father had decided to join her. He hadn't been crazy about the idea of her being down here alone. The neighborhood had changed and the locks on the back door were seriously outdated.

She'd grimaced when she'd seen them tonight. A first-grader with a bobby pin could have the door open in under fifteen seconds.

She waited for another sound, but heard nothing. After a few long moments, she sank back into the chair, doing her best to focus, but having no luck.

Trouble remained standing, the short hairs at the top of his shoulders bristled in anticipation of a fight.

Poor thing. He'd been through so much this week. She wondered how he'd like the weather in Seattle. A bit different from Philadelphia, that was for sure.

She'd no sooner powered the adding machine back on than she heard another noise, this one very familiar. The rustling of dry cleaning bags.

Someone was moving along the far wall, under the cover of darkness, behind the massive track of finished orders, tagged, bagged and waiting for pick up.

She reached for the panic button, but hesitated without applying pressure.

Had the shock and exhaustion of the past several days caught up to her? Was her mind playing tricks?

"Hello?" she called out again. Still no reply.

Trouble's small body began to tremble. The dog knew someone was there, he sensed whoever it was, smelled him.

"Steady, boy," she said softly.

Her mother had refused to own a gun, much less keep a gun at the store. She'd seen too many other store owners injured with their own weapons. But Lily would sure as hell feel better with a weapon—any weapon—at the ready right now.

A sharp rustling sounded off to one side and the growl in Trouble's throat deepened.

As much as she wanted the dog to chase off whoever had gained entrance into the shop, she knew his size would make it too easy for the intruder to injure him—or worse.

She pushed the panic button on the store's alarm system and began a slow, methodic move toward the exit. She planned to put as much distance between her and whoever it was that lurked in the dark recesses of machinery and clothing bags.

She could be just as kick ass as the next girl, but when the opportunity for escape was as near as an exit door, Lily was a big believer in rule number one.

Get out.

Trouble, however, apparently didn't share the same belief.

He took off like a shot, into the dark depths of the store, around the equipment and underneath the bags.

Lily swore softly. Stubborn little fearless dog.

"Tr—"

She caught herself just as she was about to yell his name, giving away her position. Though, considering the fact she'd been sitting at the lone desk with one of only three lights in the shop shining down on her work area, chances were pretty good whoever was inside the store knew exactly where she was.

Lily eyed the front door and mentally swore.

Trouble.

Cam had known exactly what he was doing when he'd named the dog.

The dog's deep-throated growl sounded from across the store, immediately followed by the rustling of plastic storage bags, a scuffle, a sharp yelp and then silence.

"Trouble!"

Lily sprang into action, her feet carrying her toward the sound of the injured dog before her brain kicked into gear.

More rustling plastic and the sound of hard-soled shoes on the tile floor stopped Lily in her tracks, the noises wrapping reality around her brain. She slowed, tucking herself into a bend in the machinery.

She wouldn't do Trouble any good if she rushed to him full of emotion, not taking the time to assess the situation, assess the location of the intruder.

Where were the police? She'd pressed the panic button at least two minutes ago. What was taking so long?

The machinery lurched into motion, almost trapping Lily inside its massive mechanism. She dropped to her knees and crawled, her heart pounding in her ears.

If the intruder had been able to flip the On switch, that meant he was closer than she'd thought. She had to put distance between them, had to work her way to the door and get out.

A figure shifted from out of the racks of clothing and into position in front of the door. Damn.

Large, broad-shouldered, silhouetted by the lights outside, Lily couldn't make out a face.

"I only want to talk," he called out.

The voice pulled at her memory. A noticeable accent—slight, but there.

"My mother thought maybe you could help me. Like your sister."

Buddy Grey.

Lily's insides turned liquid. Police from here to Portland, New York, were looking for this man, yet here he stood, inside her parents' shop. Unbelievable.

"You hurt my dog." She raised her voice without moving from her position.

"That was an accident." He took a few steps toward Lily's voice and she pulled back, deeper into the store, away from the exit she wanted, but closer to the back of the shop.

She'd try the back exit into the alley. The small space had always given her the willies, but a way out was a way out. She'd take what she could get.

The overwhelming noise of the machinery pounded in her skull. If she moved any farther into the store, she'd never hear what Grey said next, yet if she stopped the machinery, he'd know exactly where she was plus he'd be able to hear her every move.

She couldn't risk it. She'd have to operate on survival instinct alone. The man might be innocent of his crimes, but after seeing the scrapbook at his mother's house, Lily had no doubt he'd killed at least once. In her heart, she knew the man wouldn't hesitate to kill again.

She scrambled away from him, weaving effortlessly

through the machinery, the racks of clothing and the presses just as she'd done all her life. Thank goodness her parents hadn't changed a thing after all of these years.

"I didn't kill your sister." Grey's voice boomed, much closer than Lily would have anticipated.

He must be paralleling her movement. Damn.

She held her ground and tried to think. Something white caught the corner of her vision and she squinted, trying to make out what the object was.

Trouble's paw.

Lily's heart lurched. Damn Buddy Grey. She didn't care who he said he had or hadn't killed, he'd shown no mercy so far tonight. He'd acted first, cruelly and coldly.

And she knew then that he hadn't come here tonight simply to talk.

He'd come here to silence her, exactly as he'd silenced her sister.

Lily had to think. Had to use her brain. There was still one way out, and she intended to make it.

"Don't even try the back door."

This time when Buddy spoke, his voice sounded from just over her shoulder.

Where in the hell was Cam?

CAM SHOOK HIS HEAD, rubbing his tired eyes as he waited for a traffic light to change. He was within a few minutes of the dry cleaning shop and he couldn't wait to see Lily.

Maybe he'd had enough of police work. Maybe he'd seen enough pain and heartache to last a lifetime. Montgomery's confession had left Cam feeling spent. How could two well-educated kids act as selfishly as Montgomery and Fitzsimmons had nineteen years ago? Sadly, similar crimes happened just about every day.

Cam needed to walk away. At least for tonight.

He needed to be with Lily, if for no other reason than to see her smile.

His cell phone rang just as he took the final turn toward the shop.

"Panic alarm at the Christides store." Vince barked out the words as soon as Cam flipped his phone open.

"How long?" Cam pressed down on the accelerator and blew through a stop sign, his heart in his throat.

"Two, three minutes."

"Automatic alarm?" Cam asked, hoping the answer would be yes. Maybe Lily had grown tired of waiting and had already locked up. Perhaps the intruder had tripped the alarm all on his own.

"Manual trigger." The flat tone of Vince's voice told Cam the two men were thinking the same thing.

Cam tossed the phone onto the passenger seat and drove, solely focused on maneuvering through the tight streets and alleys toward the store as fast as he could.

Two or three minutes were two or three minutes too many. Anything could have happened in that amount of time.

His gut caught and twisted.

Lily was a capable opponent for whatever or whoever had possessed her to push the alarm. She could take care of herself, but what if Grey had made his way back into the city undetected?

Hell, what if he'd never left?

Cam had been an idiot to tell her he'd meet her at the store, to let her go to the shop without someone with her.

He cut his headlights and slammed the car to a stop in

the alley beside the store, scrambling for cover and a clean view of the store's window.

A large figure moved beyond the glass. A man. Tall. Solidly built. Checking the street.

Cam would know his profile anywhere. He'd memorized the man's face years earlier.

Buddy Grey.

Anger and trepidation tangled in Cam's gut.

He scanned the street for any sign of approaching vehicles. Where were the first responders? Where was backup?

He couldn't wait. He had to move.

Lily was in danger, and at that moment in time, only one thing mattered. Saving Lily.

Grey rushed out of sight and Cam was in motion, barreling full speed ahead, focused on saving the woman who had become more important to him than anything else in his life.

LILY HEARD SOMETHING OUTSIDE. A car perhaps? Had the police responded? Or was her mind only imagining what it wanted to hear?

So much for a panic alarm. Or maybe the police responded in silence and she just wasn't aware of their presence?

"I never hurt your sister." Grey was still too close, even though he'd moved away after he'd heard the same noise outside.

Lily said nothing, frantically trying to formulate a plan. Was it better to pull the man out into the open and keep him talking? Or was it better to remain hidden? Relatively safe?

Footfalls sounded close by and she scrambled in the direction from which she'd just come.

She pulled herself to her feet and turned, running smack

into a wall of a man, her eyes locking with the dead gaze of Buddy Grey. Emotionless. Heartless.

How could her sister have ever looked at the man and argued for his innocence? Had she cared that much about furthering her own career that she helped turn this monster loose into society.

Lily moved to twist away, but Grey grasped her arms and held on tight.

"I didn't come here to hurt you." He spoke the words flatly, robotically, and Lily knew instantly that she was in a world of danger.

"I believe you," she lied. "And I believe your mother."

Something flashed in his eyes. Doubt? Hope?

"She told me all about how you never could have committed those murders, Buddy." Lily was babbling and she didn't care. The longer she kept talking, the longer she stayed alive. "I believe you, Buddy. Just like my sister did."

Any sign of humanity she'd spotted in Grey's eyes vanished with her last words.

She'd made a tactical error. She could read it on his face.

"Your sister never believed me." He laughed, the sound artificial and forced, as if he hadn't laughed in a very long time. "She used me for a story and I let her." He shrugged without loosening his grip on Lily. If anything, his fingers dug deeper into her skin. "Why wouldn't I? She got me out. I'm a free man."

"No," Lily did her best to sound strong and confident, but failed miserably. "I can help you, Buddy. I believe you."

He shook his head, narrowing his eyes as if he were trying to decide whether to kill her now or later.

Images of his past crimes flashed through Lily's mind and her knees went weak.

No, she willed herself. Think. Think of everything you've learned. Everything The Body Hunters have taught you.

She fought against Grey's grip, twisting to no avail. The man was huge. Too huge for her to escape physically.

If she couldn't beat him physically, she'd beat him mentally.

"I liked your scrapbook, Buddy. But I wonder what the police will make of it."

His gaze darkened. "They'll never see it. No one knows about it except you and my mother."

Lily nodded. "So you'd think, but I've actually already detailed your little collection for a lot of people, Detective Hughes included."

Anger flashed in Grey's eyes and she knew she was treading on dangerous ground.

"He wasn't quite as understanding as me," she continued. "If you leave now, Buddy, you can still get away. I'll help make them believe you. I'll tell them how you spared me. They'll never know you were here."

Sirens sounded in the distance, drawing nearer.

"What did you do?" He spoke so forcefully he spit out the words.

"I pressed the panic alarm." At that point, she decided her line of bull was failing miserably. She might as well use the truth. "The store's probably surrounded by police right now."

Grey twisted one arm behind her back and walked her toward the back of the shop. Adrenaline and desperation surged inside her as she scanned the walls, the racks, the worktables, searching for a weapon. Something, anything she could use to free herself from this man.

And then she wondered if this was how Nicole had felt in the moments before her death.

"I'm not going to let you kill me," Lily said without emotion.

Grey came to a standstill then, turning her around to face him, pulling her so near she could smell his filthy clothes.

"That's where you're wrong." He pulled her up onto her tiptoes. "You're not the one in control."

CAM HAD MORE TROUBLE with the shop's back door than he'd anticipated. Grey had done something to jam the mechanism, but with a bit of work, he'd still been able to get inside.

He could make out voices from farther inside the shop. One deep. One barely audible.

Lily.

Relief washed through him. She was still alive.

He'd called again for backup before he stepped inside and silenced his phone. He couldn't risk giving away his presence or his position. If he wanted to save Lily, he had to take Grey by complete surprise.

The man had always been fond of knives, and the last thing Cam needed was for Grey to make a sudden move against Lily when Cam wasn't close enough to protect her.

He moved slowly and methodically into the store, through the back room and into the shop itself.

"I'm not going to let you kill me."

Lily's voice. Much closer than Cam had anticipated.

They were moving this way.

"That's where you're wrong."

Grey's voice.

Cam's blood ran cold, then hot, infused with anger. He'd never wanted to hear Grey's voice outside the walls of a jail cell again.

If his instincts were correct, they stood just on the other

side of the door. Cam needed only one smooth move to take Grey down. He had to trust Lily to react fast enough to get out of the way.

"You're not the one in control."

Grey's voice again. Then sirens.

Cam rushed forward, slamming the back room door outward, clipping Grey on the shoulder.

The big man stumbled and Lily made her move, hitting the ground and scrambling out of reach.

Grey spun on Cam, but froze when he spotted the barrel of Cam's revolver, pointed at the furrowed skin between the murderer's eyes.

"It's over, Grey. Again."

But apparently Grey had no intention of going down without a fight. He spun on one heel, taking off in a dead sprint toward the front of the store. Cam gave pursuit, but couldn't risk a shot, not without knowing exactly where Lily was and not without knowing whether or not other officers had taken up positions out front.

He needn't have worried.

Vince stood at the front of the store, surrounded by a small army of armed responders, all with weapons pointed and waiting for Grey to make a move.

The big man knew when he was beat. And as he was cuffed and taken away, Vince shot Cam an angry glare. "Whatever happened to waiting for your backup?"

Cam didn't stick around long enough to answer. He had other things to do.

"Lily? Where are you?"

"Over here."

He found her huddled over Trouble's limp body and he grimaced. Damn Grey. What had he done?

Lily lifted frightened eyes to Cam. "He's still breathing. Please. We have to get him help."

"What happened?" Cam dropped to her side, brushing a strand of hair from her face.

"He tried to defend me."

Cam couldn't tear his eyes from Lily's face, amazed at how relieved he felt at the sight of her. His fingers lingered on her cheek and their eyes held. "You're okay?"

She nodded. "You?"

"I'm much better now." He took off his shirt and bundled Trouble gently into his arms, wrapping him tightly to help prevent any additional shock.

As he pushed to his feet, Lily reached for his arm, squeezing his elbow. "Cam?"

He looked down at her, his stomach catching at the mix of gratitude and desire painted across her face. "Yeah."

"Thanks."

He leaned his forehead against hers. "Just doing my job."

"So you keep telling me."

Chapter Fourteen

Body Clock: 129:00

Hours later, The Body Hunters sat in the safe house kitchen, working through the pieces of the puzzle.

Lily had been checked out by emergency personnel at the scene and had insisted on getting back to work. To the naked eye, she appeared strong and resilient. To anyone who knew her well, she appeared shaken to the core.

Cam decided at that moment he knew her well. He could see right through the emotional walls she'd erected. For a fleeting moment he wondered if she could see through his.

Something about her had breached his perimeter, that was for certain.

He'd gone back to the precinct briefly to witness Buddy Grey's intake, but as much as seeing Buddy back behind bars had been his primary goal a few days ago, tonight his goal had been getting back to Lily as quickly as he could. Even though he'd spoken to her by phone from the station, he'd needed to see her with his own eyes.

He'd needed to see *her,* period.

That was a mind-numbing concept for Cam, and he wasn't sure how or when it had happened.

Buddy Grey continued to insist he was innocent in the killing of Lily's sister. He had confessed to the killing of Claire Mooney, however. Intense questioning could do that to a man.

It helped that Buddy had been overwrought by his release back into society. Seven years was a long time behind bars when you were turned loose with nothing more than pocket cash and your freedom.

At first, he'd been dismayed by how quickly everyone had forgotten his face and his name. Then after Nicole's murder, he hadn't been safe anywhere. He hadn't even been able to go home.

Sure, he'd communicated with his mother using a go-between. That's how he'd learned about Lily's visit, and he thought she might be able to help him. But she hadn't believed him. He'd realized that just before he'd decided to kill her. Five more minutes and Cam would have been too late.

The investigative team felt certain Buddy's confession to Nicole's murder would come.

Cam wasn't so certain.

He'd spent a lot of hours with Buddy Grey over the years. During his original investigation. During his arrest. During his interrogation and conviction.

But tonight at the station, something had been different.

Cam had always needed just one look to know Grey had been guilty of the trio of murders. Just as Cam had looked into Grey's eyes tonight and known the man had killed Claire Mooney. Lily had been right.

But when questioned about Nicole's murder, Grey's eyes had given off a different emotion.

Confusion. Pain. Sadness.

The former murderer might have been angry at Nicole for rushing him back out in the world unprepared, but had he killed her?

And if he hadn't killed her, who had?

"Maybe you're reading him incorrectly," Rick Matthews said as Cam finished summarizing Grey's interrogation for the group.

Cam shook his head. "I don't think so."

"But the rest of your team?"

Cam shrugged. "You're right. They think he's guilty."

"Maybe you're too close." Lily spoke the words softly, as if she knew a lack of objectivity was his worst fear.

Cam hesitated for a moment. Was he reading Grey incorrectly? Had his feelings for Lily thrown his instincts off kilter? "Maybe I'd feel differently if he confessed, but his profession of innocence seems heartfelt."

He leaned forward. "Plus, whoever killed Nicole strangled her first. Grey's murders were always about control. His satisfaction came from making his victims suffer. Nicole's murder lacked that."

Lily's gaze dropped to her lap and she pressed her lips into a tight line, as if trying to keep herself from crying out.

"Damn," Cam murmured softly. He was an idiot. "I'm sorry."

Her damp eyes lifted to his and held. "I just want it to be over."

"It will be." Cam rounded the table, taking her hands in his.

"It's late." Rick's voice broke through Cam's thoughts. For a moment, he'd forgotten any of the other team members sat in the room. As they said their good nights and left, Cam's focus returned to Lily.

She looked more shaken, more fragile, than he'd ever seen her. He also knew her well enough to know that if he voiced that thought, she'd be angry with herself for letting any sign of weakness show.

"Come on." He anchored an arm around her waist and helped her to her feet. "You need to sleep."

She nodded, saying nothing as they walked slowly back to her bedroom. She leaned her weight against him, and Cam marveled for a split second about how perfectly they fit together, bodies pressed one against the other.

They'd barely crossed the threshold into the bedroom when Lily's stoic resolve gave way. She turned into Cam, wrapping her arms around his waist as she buried her head against his chest.

He held her, the move so natural he felt as if he'd held her countless times before. And yet, at the same time, the feel of her in his arms was like coming home for the first time.

Her body shook as she let the tears come. Cam stroked her back and pressed his lips to her hair.

She needed this. Needed the release. She'd been fighting to keep her emotions under control since the moment they first met. Cam had admired her for it. But tonight…tonight she needed to cry. He was humbled by the fact she felt safe enough to let down her guard in his company.

He held her close, shifting her toward the bed, sitting beside her, not letting go for a moment.

He whispered reassurances, holding her in the darkened room, promising her he'd make everything all right.

For the briefest moment, Cam flashed on a memory of

holding his daughter, Annie, years ago in her darkened bedroom as a spring storm raged outside.

He'd promised her he'd always take care of her, always keep her safe. And yet, he hadn't kept that promise. He hadn't fought for the right to see her, to be with her, to love her.

Perhaps the time had come to take his life back. To fight for the things he loved.

The hour was too late to call his ex-wife now, even with the time difference between the coasts, but he'd call tomorrow. He'd harbored the thought many times before, but this time was different. This time, he was ready.

Falling for Lily had brought him back to life.

Falling for Lily.

The realization shook him to the core.

She shifted in his arms as her crying eased, putting a bit of space between them.

Cam looked down into her dark eyes rimmed with wet lashes, and pressed a kiss to her forehead.

"You are the most beautiful thing I've ever seen."

She laughed through her tears, shaking her head. "You should have seen my sister." Her words came on a whisper. "She was beautiful."

He nodded. "She was. But she had nothing on you."

He cupped her chin in his fingers, lowering his mouth to hers, yet holding back from kissing her.

"We don't have to do this."

"Please—" Lily pressed a finger to his lips "—I want to feel something other than loss."

She moved her finger long enough to kiss him, the sensation of her lips against his heating his insides to the boiling point.

She pulled back, inhaling sharply. "Cam…"

He studied her, waiting for the rest of whatever it was she'd been about to say, all the while wanting nothing more than to kiss her again. "What is it?"

"Just this." She smiled as she pressed her lips to his, setting off a chain reaction of awakening inside him.

How could his emotions swing so quickly from pure protectiveness to blatant desire?

Lily nipped at his lower lip then pressed her tongue between his lips, opening his mouth to hers.

That was how, he thought.

He shifted her onto his lap, gripping her waist, pulling the soft curves of her body flush against his chest. He hardened instantly, filled with a sense of urgency like none he'd ever known.

He needed Lily and he needed her now, but he didn't want to rush, didn't want to make her do anything she wasn't ready for.

"We don't have to do this," he said again softly against her mouth.

Lily feathered kisses along the side of his jaw to his neck, then sat back, unbuttoning his shirt. "Yes we do," she said. Then she cupped his chin, tipping his gaze to hers. "I need to do this, Cam. I need to do this with you."

He couldn't have summed up his own feelings any better.

She slid his shirt over his shoulders and down his arms, tracing one finger down the center of his chest to the waist-band of his jeans as he shrugged out of his sleeves.

He reached for the hem of her T-shirt, hoisting the material up and over her slender body, smiling to himself as she held her arms over her head to make his job easier.

She closed her eyes and breathed out a sigh as she lowered her arms to his shoulders, entwining her fingers into the hair at the base of his neck. "I've wanted to do this almost since the first time you copped an attitude with me."

Cam studied the lines of her body, the swell of her breasts beneath the satiny fabric of her bra. He raked a thumb across her lower lip, then hooked a finger beneath one bra strap.

"I find it difficult to believe I ever copped an attitude with you."

"Oh—" Lily tipped back her head, arching toward him as he slid first one bra strap and then the other off of her shoulders "—you most certainly did."

He pulled her even more tightly against him, pressing the heat of her body against his erection. Her breath caught and he reached behind her back to free the clasp of her bra, exposing her full beauty.

He cupped her breasts, savoring the weight of them in his palms, taking first one nipple and then the other into his mouth. He drank deeply, sucking, tasting, losing himself in the sensation of heat and need coiling deep inside him.

Lily's breath came in quick pants and she tightened her legs around him, pressing herself to him. He rolled her onto her back, lowering her to the bed as he traced a path down her bare skin to the waistband of her jeans.

He unbuttoned the denim and lowered the zipper, sliding the fabric over her hips and down her legs. Lily wiggled free as he reached for the band of her panties, dipping his finger beneath the elastic to slide them out of his way, filled with a heady sensation of power as Lily responded to his touch.

"Cam." Her soft voice broke through the spell she'd cast over him. "I need you."

He repositioned himself, kissing her deeply, cradling her face in his palms.

Beautiful. She was so beautiful.

"Make me feel alive, Cam. Please."

The echo of pain and loss in her voice reached inside him and shattered any lingering fears he had about making love to her.

He'd fought so hard not to cross this line, but there was no going back. Whether or not they made physical love no longer mattered. Something had happened between them this week, a connection he couldn't explain, a bond he knew she felt as strongly as he felt it.

They needed each other. And neither of them would ever be the same.

He moved away from the bed, unfastening his jeans and stepping free of the material and his boxers in one swift motion. This time when he lowered himself onto the bed, he rolled Lily on top, almost losing control when her long legs wrapped around his waist.

He gripped her hips, ready to guide her into position when she surprised him, sliding lower, pressing a soft kiss to his mouth before she trailed her lips to his neck, to his chest, then lower still.

THE HEAT BETWEEN LILY'S LEGS threatened to explode.

She'd hoped making love to Cam would make her feel alive, but she'd never expected this level of intensity. Her body hummed with excitement, her every nerve ending aware of this man, wanting this man.

His skin.

His lips.

His hair.

His voice.

His touch.

She wanted to experience all of him. Every inch he had to offer.

She trailed kisses down his chest, savoring every taste of him, every sinewy inch of strength and male hardness. She followed the flat plane of his belly, then reached for him, her pulse quickening at the feel of his hard length beneath her touch. The realization she'd caused his body's reaction filled her with a heady sense of empowerment.

She closed her lips over his erection, taking him slowly into her mouth, thrilling to the moan that escaped from his throat, knowing she and she alone had ratcheted up his desire.

Cam reached for her, pulling her toward him until their gazes locked and held.

"Lily, I've wanted you for so long I can't survive that sort of pressure."

She grinned, filled with a devilish sense of strength. He gripped her hips, easing his hard length inside her, keeping his gaze focused solely on her eyes.

Lily gasped at the sensation of pressure and fullness as she lowered herself over him, her entire body screaming to life. His own awareness played out in the depths of his gaze, the urgency in his expression deepening.

For the first time in days…no, years, she felt alive. Truly alive.

They moved together, their bodies joined, gazes locked, slowly at first then more quickly, moving to their shared rhythm, each anticipating the other's moves, the other's needs.

Cam slid his hands from her hips to her buttocks, pulling her tightly against him, deepening their joining. A sensation of heat burst inside her and spread, numbing every inch of her body as she cried out, the first orgasm crashing over her, taking her by surprise with its sheer intensity.

Cam pushed her further, pressing her to him even more tightly as he slowed their rhythm.

Another wave of release hit her, pulsing through her body as she cried out. Tears shimmered in her vision, tears of joy—joy at feeling after so many years of feeling nothing.

She'd feared herself dead inside. Making love to Cam had proved otherwise.

He rolled on top of her, shifting her against the soft support of the mattress, never breaking their connection. He wrapped her legs around his waist, coming up on his knees to drive so deeply inside her she thought she might splinter apart.

He moaned as his body pulsed with release, his uninhibited loss of control bringing her to yet another peak of pleasure.

They rocked together until they were fully spent, falling onto their sides, laughing, breathing heavily, stroking each other's faces with nothing but trust shimmering in their stares.

Lily lost herself in the comfort of Cam's arms, savoring the feel of her body pressed to his. Warmth seeped through every inch of her body, and the shock and grief of the past week faded into the background, chased away by the gentleness of Cam's loving touch.

She knew the sun would rise in a few hours, bringing with it the reality of all that had happened. But, for the moment, she was safe. She was protected. She was lost, sheltered inside the arms of the man she'd fallen for completely, even though she'd tried so very hard not to.

In that moment, Lily knew she'd landed exactly where she belonged—safe inside the comfort of Cam's embrace.

He stirred beside her, shifting her more closely against him. "You all right?"

Lily closed her eyes, savoring the feel of him beside her. "Perfect. I'm perfect."

And for the moment, she was.

THE MAN SAT OUTSIDE of Nicole Christides's brownstone, watching the empty house and cursing the darkness.

Surely the sister would come. After all, the danger had passed.

He tossed back his head and laughed, enjoying his own joke. His laughter reverberated loudly off the closed windows of his sedan and he forced himself to regain control.

Control.

He'd focused his life on control.

He would always focus his life on control.

Everything he'd planned so far had played out beautifully. Eliminating Lily Christides would be no different.

He reached for the floral arrangement he'd set on the passenger seat and hoped Lily arrived before her flowers wilted.

He intended to let her enjoy her flowers before he killed her. Poor Nicole hadn't lived long enough to appreciate the basket he'd bought for her. But Lily...

He planned to savor his time with Lily.

After all, he felt like he knew her now.

He pulled a daisy from the arrangement and smiled, plucking a single petal.

"She lives." He plucked another petal. "She dies."

He laughed again, this time letting himself enjoy the knowledge that soon this particular chapter in his life would be over. Then he could move on.

Another petal. "She lives."

He glanced up at the darkened house, down at his knife, and then he sighed. Lily Christides was going to die.

He'd already picked the *where* and the *how*. All that remained to be seen was the *when*.

And something told him that would be soon.

Very soon.

The Man picked one last petal.

"She dies."

Chapter Fifteen

Lily woke a few hours later, feeling rested for the first time since the nightmare of Nicole's murder began.

Cam slept, his dark lashes splayed against his cheeks. His typically intense features softened by their lovemaking.

She traced a finger over his hairline and down his cheek. He smiled and her heart warmed.

She'd be going back to Seattle soon. What then? What would become of the bond she'd forged with this man, once so arrogant and now...

Thoughts failed her.

He'd become an integral part of her life. The first person she thought of in the morning. The last person she thought of at night.

Had she fallen for him? Or had the investigation into Nicole's death shifted her perspective simply because she'd spent so much time with the man?

She silently slipped into her clothes, pulling on the jeans and shirt she'd worn the night before. Then she left Cam a note.

Lily had something to face today. Something she'd avoided thus far.

She stole one last glance at Cam's sleeping form as she sneaked out the door. She'd have to face him sooner or later. She couldn't hide forever. But for now, she knew her limits, and knew the myriad thoughts swirling through her mind needed time to settle down.

Settle down.

The words danced through her mind and she shivered, pushing them back.

She needed good, hard physical work to help clear her head, and she knew just where to get it.

She passed Martin on her way out. "I'll be at Nicole's if anyone needs me."

There were some things a parent shouldn't have to face.

Packing up a murdered daughter's belongings was one of them.

LILY WAS GONE IN THE MORNING when Cam woke.

He laughed inwardly as he read her note. Wasn't that just like the woman? She hadn't even let him be the one to sneak out.

He'd barely stepped back into his jeans when his cell phone rang.

He glanced at the display before he answered. Vince.

"We got him." Vince's words snapped across the line. "Full confession."

Cam squinted, willing his brain to focus, working to shake off the happy fog lovemaking and a good night's sleep had left behind. "Grey?"

"Described the Christides killing in detail. Right down to the call from Lily."

Cam blinked, his gut and his brain doing battle. "What about Nicole's cell phone? The weapon?"

"Said he threw both in the Schuylkill."

"What about wherever he stopped before he sent the text?"

"Said he had a drink. We're checking out that story now. It's over. This time he's going away for good."

They ended their call and Cam sank onto the edge of the bed.

This time he's going away for good.

The words should've filled Cam with a sense of satisfaction, but they did anything but.

Grey's confession didn't feel right. Cam hadn't been there, no doubt about that, but hearing Vince recount what had happened left Cam feeling oddly like he'd just listened to a script. As if Buddy had been told what to say.

But by whom?

Something deep inside his mind clicked and he bolted across the bedroom floor. He was downstairs and in the case room in a matter of seconds.

Silvia sat sipping a cup of coffee, stitching on Nicole's quilt. "Good morning, Detective."

But Cam barely heard her. Instead, he crossed to where the computer worked tirelessly to fill in the features of the photograph from Gladys Sizemore's house.

Tracey Sizemore's image had become even sharper, but the boy with her had yet to come into focus. His side of the photo had been heavily damaged, and Cam wondered if they'd ever be able to make an identification.

One name from the Camp Providence list haunted Cam, toyed with him, teased at his brain.

Bobby Grey.

What if he hadn't fallen off the face of the earth? What if he'd somehow been under their noses all along?

Cam plucked the snapshot from the wall and held it next to the computer image. There wasn't enough clarification on the screen to know whether or not the two matched, but Cam's gut told him they would.

His gut also told him that Bobby Grey had played a role in the death of Tracey Sizemore.

"Can't we speed this up?" He turned to ask Silvia, but she'd already moved next to him, studying the images alongside him. "Can we focus more narrowly?" Cam pulled an idea out of the air. "How about his eyes? Can we zero in on his eyes?"

"I'll change the program right now," a sleepy Martin said from just behind Cam's shoulder. "What's up?"

"Call it a hunch." Cam thrust the snapshot into Martin's hand. "The sooner the better, and thanks." He tipped his chin toward the photograph. "Can I get a copy of that to take with me?"

A few minutes later he was out the door, doing something he should have done before now. Why hadn't he thought of it?

Because he was distracted by his feelings for Lily, no doubt.

He pictured the love he'd seen on the team members' faces the night before as they'd surrounded Lily following her attack.

He pictured Silvia's concentration as she stitched on Nicole's quilt.

These were people who loved Lily as she deserved to be loved.

Did he love her the same way? Was he even capable of loving her the same way?

His gut caught and twisted. Truth was, he didn't know. His track record in that department left a lot to be desired.

But while he might not be able to love her, he could give her the truth. He could give her closure.

That much, he was sure of.

THE MAN CRADLED THE BASKET of flowers in one arm as he climbed the brick steps.

Lily's rental car sat out front. She must have sneaked past him while he slept.

She'd come back to the scene of the crime, just as he'd known she would. He'd imagine she felt safe now that Buddy was behind bars where he belonged.

She felt safe.

He hoped she'd like her flowers. He'd gone to a different florist this time. After all, he wouldn't want to be recognized.

Anger tapped at the base of his brain.

He'd worked his whole life to be recognized and now he had to worry about remaining forgettable. That would change soon. Soon enough.

The Man bit back another laugh, working to keep quiet as he reached for the bell.

He didn't want to startle Lily. Not yet.

There'd be plenty of time for that soon.

LILY HAD JUST PACKED UP the last of the books from Nicole's office when the doorbell rang.

Who on earth could that be?

She brushed at the front of her shirt and tucked her hair behind her ears as she stepped over Trouble. He'd fallen sound asleep the moment she'd tucked him into the chenille throw she'd pulled from Nicole's living room.

Her sister would have wrung her neck, but perhaps she would have understood that the dog deserved a soft bed and so much more.

He could have died trying to save Lily. The veterinarian had said it was nothing short of a miracle that he'd suffered a broken leg, major bruising and nothing worse.

The doorbell sounded a second time as Lily neared the front door. Surprise filtered through her when she peered through the peephole.

Handsome man. Her mother's voice from the day of the funeral rang in Lily's ears.

Handsome, yes, but what on earth was he doing here?

She pulled the door open and pasted on a smile, hoping her confusion wasn't plastered across her face. "Good morning. This is a surprise."

He smiled without saying a word, and something clicked in Lily's brain.

His eyes. What was it that was so familiar about his eyes?

"When I read the headline in the paper this morning, all I could think was how tragic it would have been if anything had happened to you." He shifted the basket of flowers he held from one arm to the other.

An odd chill gripped the back of Lily's neck and squeezed.

The headline.

His voice. She knew his voice.

Puzzle pieces flew into place in her mind.

The killer's voice. The resemblance to Buddy Grey. The eyes in the snapshot of Bobby Grey. Nicole's calls to city hall. The flowers.

Flowers. I'll call you back, Lil.

Nicole's last words rang in her brain.

From down the hall, Trouble began to growl.

Lily pushed at the door, trying to shut the man out of her sister's house, but he was bigger and faster. The basket of flowers tumbled down the brick steps to the sidewalk below and he rushed forward, knocking Lily to the tiled foyer.

She scrambled to get away, but he was on top of her, crushing her against the unforgiving floor. As he closed his fingers around her throat, Lily could only think of one thing.

If she was about to relive her sister's dying moments, she was sure as hell going to go down fighting.

Chapter Sixteen

Cam drove toward Langston Montgomery's residence. A call to the precinct had confirmed that the man had been released on bail, wearing a house arrest anklet in return for his promise to lead investigators to Tracey Sizemore's body later that day.

Cam pulled to the curb down the street from the majestic Montgomery home, marveling at the fact no reporters or news vans sat parked in the street, waiting to accost the family.

Word must not have leaked yet about the man's release.

Cam moved quickly, climbing the steps and ringing the bell. He'd told no one where he was headed, not even Vince.

At the rate things were going, this case would cost him his job, but suddenly the truth had become more important to Cam than his detective's shield.

He never would have believed himself capable of harboring that thought.

"You shouldn't be here," Montgomery said as he ushered Cam into a large study. He poured himself a cup of coffee, offering none to Cam.

Langston's wife and small children had made themselves scarce upon Cam's arrival.

"My lawyer has instructed me to say nothing about the case," Montgomery continued, pacing in the spacious room.

"I'm sure he has." Cam sank onto the deep leather sofa, sitting back and relaxing, not waiting for an invitation. "And my lieutenant would croak if he knew I was here with you, so let's keep this off the record and just between you and me. Sound good?"

Montgomery frowned. "What purpose will that serve?"

Cam had never liked the mayor, and now he knew why. The man appeared perpetually nervous. It was as if he were constantly waiting for the other shoe to drop. But then, Cam realized, he had been waiting. For nineteen years.

"Who else was there that day?" Cam asked.

Montgomery breathed in sharply. "No one."

"I know you're lying and you know you're lying." Cam leaned forward, elbows to knees, chin on fists. "You're protecting someone and I want to know who."

For a split second, Montgomery looked like a deer caught in the headlights, a frightened, cornered animal.

"The phone call records suggest you killed both Tim and Gladys Sizemore." Cam laced his fingers behind his head and sat back. "I just can't picture you pulling the trigger or killing that kind woman, though, can you? I mean look at you. You're scared of *me*."

He forced himself to remain seated when all he wanted to do was spring across the room and pin Montgomery to the wall.

"I need you to leave now, Detective." Montgomery made a move toward the door, anger flashing in his eyes.

"Who is it?" Cam asked without standing. "Another camper? Did someone see you kill the Sizemore girl?"

The color drained from Montgomery's face. "Who told you that?"

Cam smiled, pushing to his feet. "You just did."

Panic flashed in Montgomery's eyes and a picture solidified in Cam's mind. "Someone saw you and blackmailed you. Is that right?"

The other man said nothing, not moving an inch.

Cam barreled ahead. "I'd imagine he would have used your connections to make a nice life for himself, or was it simply money he was after?"

Montgomery's throat worked.

"You don't really need to answer that one—" Cam shook his head "—I happen to know someone who's quite adept at tracing financial records."

"I never paid anyone." Montgomery's voice tightened.

"But you helped someone? Someone who still obviously holds quite a bit of control over you."

Montgomery breathed in and out loudly. "You should leave now."

Cam crossed the room, taking in the expansive bookcase. Just like Tim Fitzsimmons, the outgoing mayor's shelves were covered with awards and photographs.

Cam focused on the photos, studied each face, doing his best to calculate how long Montgomery would have known each person.

He pulled the photo of Bobby Grey from his pocket, thrusting it toward Montgomery. "Did he see what you did? Did he help? Did you pose him just like you posed Tracey? Or are you protecting him even now?"

Montgomery's anger broke, spilling out in a barrage of

words. "I'm not protecting him. I'd never protect him. I hope he burns in hell."

His features shifted from angry to guilty, as if the part of him so used to lying refused to give up control to the part of him that now wanted to come clean.

He turned away.

Cam dropped his gaze to the photograph of Bobby Grey, seeing something he hadn't seen there before.

He snatched a framed photo from the shelf and held the two images side by side.

The eyes were the same.

How had he missed this?

The man's eyes were emotionless. Cold.

A dead match.

Silvia continued her work on Nicole's quilt while she kept an eye on the photo restoration process. She'd wanted to finish Nicole's quilt in time for the funeral, but these things took time.

She glanced up at the screen and blinked. Cam's idea had worked. The eyes of the young man had become sharper, almost recognizable.

The program made another pass and then beeped.

Silvia's breath caught.

She put down her stitching and walked closer to the screen, tipping her head to one side as she searched her memory.

She'd seen those eyes somewhere before.

She held Bobby Grey's photo to the screen and saw the match instantly. But she knew there was more.

The eyes were cold, calculating, and she'd seen them recently. But where? Who?

She buzzed up to the kitchen and Kyle and Rick were at her side in no time.

"Bobby Grey." Rick whistled the instant he looked at the screen.

"But we know him as someone else." Silvia traced a finger across the image. "Someone we've seen here. In Philadelphia."

"You don't see it?" Martin spoke from the doorway, his tone off—scared, surprised.

He crossed the room, pointing to the eyes. "Picture him older. Twenty years older. Then think about the funeral. Process every face you saw."

Kyle and Rick made the connection first. Silvia took a few extra seconds to wrap her brain around the reality of what she was seeing.

Her heart beat so quickly she thought she might be sick. "Where did Lily go?"

"To her sister's to pack."

Kyle and Rick were out the door in an instant, running fast.

Silvia dialed Lily's cell but got no answer, then she sank into a chair and did the only thing she felt capable of doing at a time like this.

She prayed.

"He said he'd kill my family."

Montgomery spoke the words in a low whisper. Cam's blood ran cold as he stared down into the trio of faces. Fitzsimmons was a non-entity, as was Montgomery. It was the third pair of eyes staring back on which Cam focused.

Too bad Nicole hadn't lived to see her own story through. This headline was going to be bigger than anything Philadelphia had seen in decades.

"We can protect your wife and your children until we get him in custody. Come back to the station and make a full confession this time."

"He's too smart. You'll never find a thing on him."

"I'd say your word is enough, Mayor Montgomery."

"I made him a very powerful man." Montgomery's words dripped with bitterness and shame.

"No one forced you to do anything, sir."

Montgomery nodded as Cam turned to meet his stare. "He did." The other man tapped the face in the picture frame. "He said he'd destroy me. Destroy my family."

Montgomery dropped his voice to a whisper. "He said he'd slice up my wife just like he sliced up Nicole."

Cam winced as he reached for his phone. So he'd been right about Buddy Grey's confession. He'd been told exactly what to say by his younger brother, Nicole's real killer.

"You knew he'd killed her and you didn't come forward?"

"I thought it would be over then." Montgomery stared at the face in the photograph, the face of evil. "It's never going to be over."

"Yes, it is." Cam launched himself into motion, dialing his cell phone as he ran. He needed to get Montgomery and his family to a safe location, and he needed to reach Lily.

He dialed her Body Hunters cell phone but his call went instantly into voice mail.

"I know who killed your sister," he barked out. "Do not. I repeat, do not leave Nicole's. And don't open that door for anyone but me."

His next call was to Rick's cell phone. The agency co-director answered on the first ring, his greeting on the breathless side.

Cam didn't have time to ask what was wrong. "I know who killed Nicole."

"And we know who Bobby Grey is."

Both men said the same name at the same moment, then swore loudly.

"We'll be at the brownstone in ten minutes," Rick said.

"I can be there in five." Cam cranked on his ignition.

"She's not answering her cell."

"I know." Cam steeled himself, determined to save the woman he loved. "I'm calling for backup."

He disconnected the call and dialed the precinct as he screamed the tires away from the curb in front of the Montgomery mansion, pushing his car to its breaking point.

Five minutes later, he skidded to a stop in front of Nicole's brownstone. What he saw there stopped him cold.

A basket of flowers lay at the bottom of the brick steps, broken, discarded, forgotten.

His cell phone rang and he answered.

"We can't locate Patterson." Anxiety screamed through Vince's voice.

Fear and determination wrapped themselves around Cam's heart as he launched himself from the car.

"I think I know exactly where to find him."

LILY FOUGHT TO SCRAMBLE OUT from beneath Ross Patterson's weight. She shoved the base of her palm at his face, connecting solidly with his nose. He rolled away from her, giving her enough time to scramble to her feet.

Trouble charged from down the hall, hobbling on three legs.

Fury blazed to life in Patterson's eyes, and he pulled a knife from the back of his waistband.

"I hate that dog. I should have killed him when I had a chance."

Trouble showed no sign of slowing down and Lily was not about to watch the dog meet his end at the tip of Patterson's knife.

She lunged, wincing as her forearm connected with the blade, sending it clattering across the floor. Pain blossomed and spread, but she kept her eyes focused solely on Patterson, not on her wound.

He gripped her tightly, slamming her body against the wall.

"Damn you Christides women."

Lily's brain operated at warp speed, her mind trying to process what was happening at the same time the pieces of the mystery snapped into place.

She'd turned off her cell phone. Idiot. Wanting quiet in which to honor the sanctity of packing away her sister's life.

Trouble attacked, barking and snarling, winding himself between Patterson's feet and her feet, taking the two of them down in a heap.

"No," she yelled as Patterson swung a fist at the dog.

Trouble leaped into the air and came down snarling, sinking his fangs into Patterson's wrist. If Lily didn't know better she'd swear the dog was part Pit Bull, but Trouble wasn't able to withstand Patterson's strength.

His body flew through the air, hitting the wall with a sickening thud.

Patterson seized the opportunity to solidify his attack on Lily, using the distraction to slam her against the floor. Hard.

Her vision swam, stars dancing in her line of sight.

She had to stay alive. Had to survive until Cam got here, and somehow she knew he would. She could feel him, feel his sense of urgency.

He'd figure out the killer's identity, just as she'd figured it out.

He had to.

She tried to move, but couldn't. Her body had been so battered and bruised that her muscles wouldn't respond to her brain's command to run.

Patterson scrambled to his feet, slamming the front door and flipping the dead bolt.

"I thought I'd take a little more time with you than I did with your sister." His heartless tone reacted inside her and twisted. "She wasn't my best effort, even though I'm not as practiced at this as my brother is."

"Buddy?" she asked, suddenly realizing she could perhaps keep him talking.

She was able to pull herself to an upright position, bracing herself against the wall. The room spun black momentarily, but righted itself, just in time for her to focus on Patterson's face, mere inches from hers.

He held up a length of cord, grinning as he reached first for her feet and then for her hands. "I find it easier to work if I have a captive audience, so to speak."

"Did you learn that from Montgomery and Fitzsimmons?"

He laughed, the sound cold and terrifying. "They didn't kill that girl, they only thought they did. I took care of it, though."

One brow lifted toward his perfect hairline. "I rather enjoyed taking her life. I liked the control, the power, the high. I think that was the first time I ever truly understood what drove my brother to kill."

Anger and disgust surged inside Lily, but she tamped both down, battling to stay focused, to stay conscious, to stay alive.

"And then you vanished?"

Patterson shook his head, tightening the cord around her ankles. "Then I was reborn. New name. New life. New world."

"Until my sister came along."

He nodded. "It was my pleasure to kill that bitch."

Lily wanted to kick him, wanted to curse him, wanted to rip his eyes out, but at that moment, her mind and body gave out, succumbing to her injuries and her loss of blood.

Her world turned black.

CAM RACED TOWARD THE FRONT door, trying the doorknob, but finding it locked up tight.

He heard voices from inside. Laughter.

Male. Evil.

Patterson.

He cupped his hands over the windows beside the door, able to make out Trouble's apparently lifeless shape and that of a man, huddled over Lily, binding her unconscious form.

His heart leaped into his throat, his gut tightening with urgency.

He wasn't about to lose Lily. Not like this.

Not to a madman like Patterson.

He unholstered his revolver and aimed at the door's dead bolt. The wood splintered an instant after he squeezed off his shot.

Cam kicked the door open, but Patterson was waiting, ready, his knife pressed to Lily's throat.

Patterson grinned, the smile of a killer. Then he laughed.

"What took you so long, Detective? I would have thought you'd figure this out days ago."

Cam let the man's words roll off his back. He had no interest in matching wits, or in hearing a detailed account of Patterson's genius. As far as he was concerned, the story was straightforward.

Patterson had blackmailed his way into power, and when his secret had begun to crumble—thanks to Nicole's investigative skills—Patterson had panicked, systematically eliminating each threat to everything he'd achieved.

Well, the elimination stopped here and now.

"Put down the knife." Cam steadied his aim.

"Or else what? You'll shoot me? Don't you think I can slice her throat in the time it takes you to pull that trigger?"

Beneath Patterson's touch, Lily stirred.

Cam silently willed her not to move, but she blinked her eyes open, the sight of her raw fear gripping Cam's gut and squeezing tight.

Her mouth moved, but Cam shook his head, signaling her to say nothing.

From behind her, Trouble whimpered.

Patterson stiffened at the noise and glanced away for the slightest moment.

Car brakes sounded outside, followed by shouting voices and countless footfalls racing toward the doorway.

Cam didn't wait for backup. Instead he seized the moment, realizing Patterson's knife had pulled away from Lily's throat just far enough to give him room.

The scene played out in slow motion, yet was over in the blink of an eye.

Cam took his shot just as Trouble sprang to life,

charging away from the wall. Lily turned her head as the knife fell from Patterson's grip.

Patterson hit the floor with a thud, almost at the same moment Cam's shot exploded through the foyer. The man gripped his knee and rolled, blood seeping between his fingers as he hurled a string of expletives at Cam, at Lily, at Rick and Kyle and Vince as they charged into Nicole's house.

Cam stripped the cords from Lily's wrists and ankles as uniformed officers took Patterson into custody. He pulled off his shirt, wrapping it around the angry knife wound on her arm, and she pressed her palm to his cheek.

Trouble circled Patterson, snarling and growling as they led the hobbling man away.

"You came for me." The trust and determination in Lily's voice captured Cam's heart and held.

"Just doing my job." He pressed a soft kiss to her forehead and then to her mouth.

"I love you, Cam."

He smiled, warmed by the variation on their usual banter. He pulled her into his arms, silently vowing to never let her go.

In Lily he'd found the one thing that had been missing from his life forever.

He'd found love.

True love.

He'd found someone with whom he wanted to share the rest of his life, no matter where that life might take them.

He cupped her chin in his fingers, wanting to make sure she looked into his eyes as he spoke the words he'd been afraid of for longer than he cared to admit.

"I love you, too."

Epilogue

For the Christides family, the Body Clock had stopped ticking in the very place where it had begun.

Nicole's home.

Under intense questioning, Ross Patterson detailed the day he'd witnessed Montgomery and Fitzsimmons with Tracey Sizemore.

His life changed the night he stumbled upon the panicked pair who would have never given him a second glance otherwise. He then held the power to destroy their charmed lives simply by telling officials what they had done.

But what Montgomery and Fitzsimmons never knew was that Ross had gone back to the hiding spot after lights out, compelled to look at the girl, to touch her. She hadn't been dead after all, but had been fighting her way out of the gully where she'd been left for dead.

Ross had taken her life with his own hands, ensuring his position of control over Fitzsimmons and Montgomery forever. Ensuring a life filled with connections and opportunities he'd never dreamed of.

When Gladys Sizemore gained renewed media attention on the fifteenth anniversary of her niece's disappearance, Ross had used a candid photograph from camp to gain the woman's trust. He'd painted himself as a friend to Tracey and he'd phoned the woman every month from that point forward.

After all, how better to remain informed of any risk to his secret than to befriend the girl's aunt.

Yet he'd miscalculated the importance of the very photo he'd used to secure the woman's trust. After all, no other proof of his attendance at Camp Providence existed. Yes, his attendance at camp would be recorded on any surviving registration list, but he'd changed his name after that fateful summer.

Exploiting Montgomery and Fitzsimmons marked the start of his new life—his life as Ross Patterson.

He'd killed Nicole after she'd visited Gladys Sizemore and questioned his resemblance to the photograph from Camp Providence. His brother's release had presented the perfect opportunity to copycat Buddy's methods.

Turned out Buddy Grey hadn't told his mother everything after all. He and his brother had kept in touch over the years, right up until the moment Ross described in detail how he'd killed Nicole. Buddy had been proud. So proud.

Yet Buddy had been so lost and unhappy in the outside world that he'd agreed to kill Lily, although he'd failed miserably that night at the dry cleaning shop. He'd redeemed himself by confessing to Nicole's murder, giving Ross ample time to take care of Lily himself.

The final autopsy report on Gladys Sizemore had supported what The Body Hunters suspected all along. Ross Patterson, a diabetic just like his mother, Dorothy, had killed Sizemore with a shot of his own insulin.

He'd never expected her to live long enough to pull his photo from the fireplace—the same photo he'd used four years earlier to gain her trust.

When Tim Fitzsimmons panicked after being questioned by Cam, Patterson had killed him in cold blood as he stood waiting in Fairmount Park for their meeting. Then he'd planted the prepaid cell phone in Montgomery's desk. After all, no one ever questioned the actions of the mayor's right-hand man.

In Patterson's mind, Lily was the last wild card standing between his murderous past and his mayoral future. But, he'd underestimated the one thing of which he had no real understanding.

The power of two people in love—the strength of a woman determined to survive and the determination of a man strong enough to save her.

As part of his plea agreement, Patterson had led police to the exact location where he'd buried Tracey Sizemore's body nineteen years earlier. The mystery of her disappearance had been solved at last.

Lily squeezed Cam's arm with her good hand as she shifted her injured arm in its protective sling.

The group gathered around the graveside was larger than she'd expected. She and Cam. The rest of The Body Hunters team. Countless uniformed officers from the city, rural and suburban precincts that had worked so hard to find justice for the Sizemore family.

Tracey Sizemore had finally come home. If only Gladys Sizemore had lived long enough to find the closure for which she'd fought for nineteen years.

Tears swam in Lily's vision as she stared at the twin caskets. Aunt and Niece. Reunited in death.

Perhaps it was better Gladys hadn't lived to know the full truth.

Perhaps the kinder fate had been dying before any remaining trace of hope in her heart had been shattered by the truth—that Tracey had survived her initial fall only to be murdered by a psychotic opportunist then known as Bobby Grey.

"You ready?" Cam wrapped his arm around her waist and tucked her against his side as the rest of the mourners began to scatter.

Lily nodded.

An amazing thing had happened.

Cam had decided to leave the force. He'd be returning with her to Seattle to start their new life...together.

She'd been ready to leave Seattle behind for the chance at a life with Cam in Philadelphia, but they'd realized they made a formidable investigative team. Just the sort of duo meant to work as part of The Body Hunters—together.

Cam had reached out to his ex-wife and his daughter. He and Lily planned to stop in Los Angeles on their way back home to pick up some very important cargo—a new batch of drawings, made especially for the loft they'd be sharing.

Every time Cam mentioned their upcoming visit with Annie, the light of excitement and love in his eyes was almost more than Lily could bear.

He'd come so far from the emotionally closed-off detective she'd met just two weeks earlier. He no longer swore each time he reached for his pack of gum, and he no longer scowled on a daily basis. And while a small part of her might miss the arrogant detective, she loved the man.

Lily pressed a kiss to his cheek.

She loved him with all of her heart. No qualms. No doubts. No fears.

Cam snapped his fingers and Trouble raced over to where they stood, amazingly agile considering his tiny cast still covered one leg.

Cam shot Lily another look. "Ready? We're going to miss our flight."

She nodded.

Was she ready?

Yes. She truly was.

And Lily realized, as she and Cam walked away from each of their old lives toward their new life together, Trouble at their feet, that she'd never been more ready for anything in her life.

* * * * *

Kathleen Long's miniseries, **THE BODY HUNTERS,**
continues next month when Kyle is reunited
with a woman from his recent past and finds her
a challenging incentive to solve a new case.
Look for UNDERCOVER COMMITMENT
only from Harlequin Intrigue.

THOROUGHBRED LEGACY
*The stakes are high when it comes to love,
horse racing, family secrets
and broken promises.*

*A new exciting Harlequin continuity series coming soon!
Led by* New York Times *bestselling author
Elizabeth Bevarly*
FLIRTING WITH TROUBLE

Here's a preview!

THE DOOR CLOSED behind them, throwing them into darkness and leaving them utterly alone. And the next thing Daniel knew, he heard himself saying, "Marnie, I'm sorry about the way things turned out in Del Mar."

She said nothing at first, only strode across the room and stared out the window beside him. Although he couldn't see her well in the darkness—he still hadn't switched on a light…but then, neither had she—he imagined her expression was a little preoccupied, a little anxious, a little confused.

Finally, very softly, she said, "Are you?"

He nodded, then, worried she wouldn't be able to see the gesture, added, "Yeah. I am. I should have said goodbye to you."

"Yes, you should have."

Actually, he thought, there were a lot of things he should have done in Del Mar. He'd had *a lot* riding on the Pacific Classic, and even more on his entry, Little Joe, but after meeting Marnie, the Pacific Classic had been the last thing on Daniel's mind. His loss at Del Mar had pretty much ended his career before it had even begun, and he'd had to start all over again, rebuilding from nothing.

He simply had not then and did not now have room in his life for a woman as potent as Marnie Roberts. He was a horseman first and foremost. From the time he was a schoolboy, he'd known what he wanted to do with his life—be the best possible trainer he could be.

He had to make sure Marnie understood—and he understood, too—why things had ended the way they had eight years ago. He just wished he could find the words to do that. Hell, he wished he could find the *thoughts* to do that.

"You made me forget things, Marnie, things that I really needed to remember. And that scared the hell out of me. Little Joe should have won the Classic. He was by far the best horse entered in that race. But I didn't give him the attention he needed and deserved that week, because all I could think about was you. Hell, when I woke up that morning all I wanted to do was lie there and look at you, and then wake you up and make love to you again. If I hadn't left when I did—the way I did—I might still be lying there in that bed with you, thinking about nothing else."

"And would that be so terrible?" she asked.

"Of course not," he told her. "But that wasn't why I was in Del Mar," he repeated. "I was in Del Mar to win a race. That was my job. And my work was the most important thing to me."

She said nothing for a moment, only studied his face in the darkness as if looking for the answer to a very important question. Finally she asked, "And what's the most important thing to you now, Daniel?"

Wasn't the answer to that obvious? "My work," he answered automatically.

She nodded slowly. "Of course," she said softly. "That is, after all, what you do best."

Her comment, too, puzzled him. She made it sound as if being good at what he did was a bad thing.

She bit her lip thoughtfully, her eyes fixed on his, glimmering in the scant moonlight that was filtering through the window. And damned if Daniel didn't find himself wanting to pull her into his arms and kiss her. But as much as it might have felt as if no time had passed since Del Mar, there were eight years between now and then. And eight years was a long time in the best of circumstances. For Daniel and Marnie, it was virtually a lifetime.

So Daniel turned and started for the door, then halted. He couldn't just walk away and leave things as they were, unsettled. He'd done that eight years ago and regretted it.

"It *was* good to see you again, Marnie," he said softly. And since he was being honest, he added, "I hope we see each other again."

She didn't say anything in response, only stood silhouetted against the window with her arms wrapped around her in a way that made him wonder whether she was doing it because she was cold, or if she just needed something—someone—to hold on to. In either case, Daniel understood. There was an emptiness clinging to him that he suspected would be there for a long time.

* * * * *

THOROUGHBRED LEGACY
coming soon wherever books are sold!

Thoroughbred *Legacy*

Launching in June 2008

A dramatic new 12-book continuity that embodies the American Dream.

Meet the Prestons, owners of Quest Stables, a successful horse-racing and breeding empire. But the lives, loves and reputations of this hardworking family are put at risk when a breeding scandal unfolds.

Flirting with Trouble

by *New York Times* bestselling author

ELIZABETH BEVARLY

Eight years ago, publicist Marnie Roberts spent seven days of bliss with Australian horse trainer Daniel Whittleson. But just as quickly, he disappeared. Now Marnie is heading to Australia to finally confront the man she's never been able to forget.

The stakes are high when it comes to love, horse racing, family secrets and broken promises.

A new exciting Harlequin continuity series coming soon!

Cole's Red-Hot Pursuit

Cole Westmoreland is a man who gets what he
wants. And he wants independent and sultry
Patrina Forman! She resists him—until a Montana
blizzard traps them together. For three delicious
nights, Cole indulges Patrina with his brand of
seduction. When the sun comes out, Cole and
Patrina are left to wonder—will this be the end of
the passion that storms between them?

Look for

COLE'S RED-HOT
PURSUIT

by USA TODAY bestselling author

BRENDA
JACKSON

Available in June 2008 wherever you buy books.

Always Powerful, Passionate and Provocative.

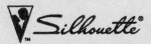

REQUEST YOUR FREE BOOKS!

2 FREE NOVELS PLUS 2 FREE GIFTS!

HARLEQUIN®
INTRIGUE®

Breathtaking Romantic Suspense

YES! Please send me 2 FREE Harlequin Intrigue® novels and my 2 FREE gifts (gifts are worth about $10). After receiving them, if I don't wish to receive any more books, I can return the shipping statement marked "cancel." If I don't cancel, I will receive 6 brand-new novels every month and be billed just $4.24 per book in the U.S. or $4.99 per book in Canada, plus 25¢ shipping and handling per book and applicable taxes, if any*. That's a savings of close to 15% off the cover price! I understand that accepting the 2 free books and gifts places me under no obligation to buy anything. I can always return a shipment and cancel at any time. Even if I never buy another book from Harlequin, the two free books and gifts are mine to keep forever.

182 HDN EEZ7   382 HDN EEZK

Name	(PLEASE PRINT)	
Address		Apt. #
City	State/Prov.	Zip/Postal Code

Signature (if under 18, a parent or guardian must sign)

Mail to the **Harlequin Reader Service:**
IN U.S.A.: P.O. Box 1867, Buffalo, NY 14240-1867
IN CANADA: P.O. Box 609, Fort Erie, Ontario L2A 5X3

Not valid to current subscribers of Harlequin Intrigue books.

Want to try two free books from another line?
Call 1-800-873-8635 or visit www.morefreebooks.com.

* Terms and prices subject to change without notice. N.Y. residents add applicable sales tax. Canadian residents will be charged applicable provincial taxes and GST. This offer is limited to one order per household. All orders subject to approval. Credit or debit balances in a customer's account(s) may be offset by any other outstanding balance owed by or to the customer. Please allow 4 to 6 weeks for delivery. Offer available while quantities last.

Your Privacy: Harlequin is committed to protecting your privacy. Our Privacy Policy is available online at www.eHarlequin.com or upon request from the Reader Service. From time to time we make our lists of customers available to reputable third parties who may have a product or service of interest to you. If you would prefer we not share your name and address, please check here. ☐

HI0

NEW YORK TIMES
BESTSELLING AUTHOR

ANNE STUART

Talk about lost in translation....

In the wake of a failed love affair, Jilly Lovitz takes off for
Tokyo. She's expecting to cry on her sister Summer's shoulder,
then spend a couple months blowing off steam in Japan.
Instead, she's snatched away on the back of a motorcycle,
narrowly avoiding a grisly execution attempt meant for her
sister and brother-in-law.

Her rescuer is Reno. They'd met before and the attraction was
odd but electric. Now Reno and Jilly are pawns in a deadly
tangle of assassination attempts, kidnappings and prisoner
swaps that could put their steamy partnership on ice.

FIRE AND ICE

"Anne Stuart delivers exciting stuff for those of us who like
our romantic suspense dark and dangerous."
—*New York Times* bestselling author Jayne Ann Krentz

*Available the first week of May 2008
wherever paperbacks are sold!*

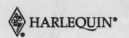